Amanda Crum
Watch for More

Novels by Amanda Crum

From Indigo Sea Press

indigoseapress.com

Ghosts of The Imperial

By

Amanda Crum

Star Crossed Books
Published by Indigo Sea Press
Winston-Salem

Amanda Crum

Star Crossed Books
Indigo Sea Press, LLC
302 Ricks Drive
Winston-Salem, NC 27103

Copyright 2015 by Amanda Crum

First Star Crossed Books edition published
December, 2015.
Star Crossed Books, Moon Sailor, and all production design are trademarks of Indigo Sea Press, used under license.

For information regarding bulk purchases of this book, digital purchase and special discounts, please contact the publisher at indigoseapress.com

Cover design by Pan Morelli

Manufactured in the United States of America
ISBN 978-1-63066-193-9

DEDICATION

Amanda Crum

Prologue
(Entry from Lucy Garside's journal)

I'm in love with a movie star.

His name is Archer Black. No matter how many times I hear that name, it creates gooseflesh on my arms.

He's beautiful, of course; his hair is wild and dark, his eyes much the same. His body could have been chiseled from marble by Michelangelo himself. His voice is like a satin sheet upon smooth skin.

He's restless when he sleeps; I have to wonder if it is this way every night. He tosses and turns in bed, thrashing the blankets around until they are a jumbled mess on the floor. His hands clench into fists until his nails cut tiny crescent shapes into his palms, and still he does not wake up. He is lost in some dream, perhaps a memory which he cannot keep in the peripheral part of his subconscious.

A little while ago I heard him say, very clearly, the name Lucy. It startled me, shook me to the core, because that is my name. But I know it was not me he was dreaming of; surely it was only some young thing who won his affections last night. It could not be my name he spoke aloud. As much as I wish it to be true, it is impossible.

Because, you see, I am dead.

I have been dead for seventy-five years. I am a ghost, in love with a living man I cannot have.

Chapter One

I was born in New York in the year 1915.

Autumn had come to the city and the trees in Greensward-- what is now known as Central Park--burned with color. My mother, Anastasia Garside, loved fall weather. She was known to take walks around the city when the air turned cool, much to the consternation of my father; it was viewed as improper for a lady to walk about unchaperoned. But my mother didn't care what others thought of her, and because my father loved her so much, and because he knew he wouldn't win an argument with her (even though he was a very successful lawyer), he let her do as she pleased most days. That is how I came to be born in a hansom cab. My mother didn't let even a painful event such as childbirth get in the way of her daily walk.

I had two sisters, one older and one younger than myself, and when we were children I thought I would never find better friends than those two. While most siblings--especially those close in age--fought like cats and dogs, the three of us only became closer the older we got. Looking back, I suppose our love for each other was born out of the necessity for a normal relationship. Our mother was busy with her society friends and with the various charities and organizations she ran. Our father, while a sweet and loving man, was also a hard worker. Most days we only saw him for a few moments in the morning and then again at dinner before he retired to his study to work on whichever case was keeping him busy at the time. From a time very early on, Emily, Elizabeth and I clung to one another like frightened children. In a way, I suppose we were just that.

But we knew our parents loved us. We were fortunate girls, living in a lovely townhouse in the city and never wanting for anything material. I suppose, if I were pressed, I would say that the only blight on my life was the loneliness that seemed to cling to my skin. Even in the presence of my sisters, the two people I loved and trusted most in the world, I felt alone. I had always viewed myself as different from most people, having a shy and artistic nature, and there were days when I felt as though I would never find someone who truly understood me.

Then, in the summer of 1930, I met someone who would change my life forever. His name was Benjamin Delacorte and his large family--he had four brothers and sisters--moved to our neighborhood after his father lost his job at one of the biggest banks in New York. They were forced to take up residence with an elderly aunt of Benjamin's in the townhouse right across from ours, and stayed there for four years despite the tight sleeping quarters. They had nowhere else to go; the Great Depression was upon us.

Ben and I became friends immediately and I discovered that we were two sides of the same coin; the two of us were alike in so many ways it was uncanny. I quickly concluded that he was my soul mate, although not in a romantic way. I was only fifteen and, while he was certainly handsome enough, I never thought of him in that light. He became so important to me in such a short amount of time that I couldn't bear the thought of ruining what we had with a relationship. Falling in love and getting married was all my sisters could think about, but at that time those things were at the farthest corners of my mind. It wasn't until I was nineteen that I began to wonder about the man I would marry and the children I would someday have, and by then it was too late.

Ben was my best friend, my other half, the brother I never had. We had conversations about important things, things that mattered; while Emily and Elizabeth only wanted to talk about fashion and which movie star they thought was the best looking, I was interested in astronomy and the latest books. The Great Gatsby became one of my favorites right after it was published in 1925, and Ben shared my love for it. We must have spent hours upon hours discussing Nick Carraway and Daisy Buchanan while sitting in Central Park, picnicking on a blanket while couples walked their dogs on the paths around us. That was just one of the many things I loved about Ben: he was well read and knew about most of the subjects that fascinated me.

3

Sometimes he would come over to the house when the weather was nice and we would lie in the small patch of grass that made up our back lawn and wait for the sun to go down, and as soon as the stars came out he would point out the constellations and tell me the story of each one. Our favorite was the myth of Castor and Pollux, the twin Greek Gods who were so close that even death couldn't keep them apart.

"That's like me and you, Luce," Ben told me once. We were lying on a blanket at dusk, enjoying a lovely Indian Summer evening. "We may not be twins, but I don't think we would let a little thing like death separate us."

"Not only are we not twins, we're also not brothers," I said, raising one eyebrow.

He flapped a hand at me dismissively. He knew I understood his comparison. We didn't need words to form an understanding about anything; we just knew.

But as much as I enjoyed spending time with him, part of me always felt guilty when I was with Ben, because my family wasn't hit nearly as hard during the Depression as his was. In fact, my sisters and I weren't really affected by the hardships at all. Our father had worked hard his entire adult life to ensure that we would be taken care of if times ever got bad. Ben, on the other hand, was sleeping in a tiny loft room with his two brothers and ate quickbread for lunch almost every day.It seemed that, without any prompting on my part, a great divide had been placed between us before our relationship was even formed, one which was unspoken and invisible but still heartily felt. It was as though our friendship, as lovely and perfect as it was, had been formed under a veil of hardship which only one of us suffered through, and was therefore made dirty and shameful. Had we met while both of us were struggling, things would have been very different, and I think we knew it.

****

"Do you think things would be better if we lived someplace else?" Ben asked me once.

Ghosts of the Imperial

It was 1933 and I was eighteen years old. The United States was much like an elderly person who had contracted a serious case of the flu but was starting to recover, slowly but surely. Our nation was by no means out of the dark, but we could see a light at the end of the tunnel. Suddenly, I started to think about the future and where life would take me in the coming years. I had so many dreams, so many things I wanted to do; I wanted to go to college, I wanted to soak up every bit of information I could. I wanted to live.

When Ben brought up the subject of moving away, we were sitting on a bench outside Mirkin's Pharmacy, sharing a Brown Cow, and I looked at him curiously over the soda glass.

"What do you mean?"

"Well, say we went out to California. People say there's gold buried in the hills there, you know. We could dig it up and sell it and then buy a farm with the money. We could grow our own vegetables and not have to worry about where our next meal is coming from. We could be done with this stinking city."

My heart broke a little for him then. Until that moment, I hadn't imagined just how bad it was for him and his family, living in a strange, cramped house with an infirm woman they barely knew. Ben had gotten a job from Mr. Keegan, the owner of our favorite little corner store, and went in four times a week to stock the shelves; but we both knew Mr. Keegan only offered him the job because he liked Ben, as most people did, and he couldn't really afford to pay him very much. Even so, Ben's paycheck was handed over to supplement his father's meager income as a typist. The whole family did their part to help out in any way they could. I remember Ben telling me that his youngest sisters, Josephine and MaryAnn, set up a lemonade stand on the sidewalk to earn money. He had smiled as he relived how they turned over their earnings for the day to their father, dumping the coins into his cupped hands, but behind the smile there was a sadness I had never seen. Before the stock market crashed, his father had been a powerful man. Now he was merely a shell of that man, a beaten-down ghost

Amanda Crum

who haunted the hallways of that old townhouse with his shirt untucked and his face bearing the stubble of a beard. Nothing would ever be the same.

"Why, Ben Delacorte, are you askin' me to run away with you?" I asked, batting my lashes dramatically.

I had meant it as a joke, but his expression was serious when he turned to look at me.

"What if I am?"

I looked into his grey-blue eyes and saw something there that scared me: Ben loved me. Really, really loved me. We had been friends for three years and I had cared for him almost immediately, but I had never wanted anything more than a friendship from him. We were too close, too much alike, and it would have been like forming a crush on my own brother. Yet I knew from the way he was looking at me that he felt differently.

"Ben," I began breathlessly, "You can't solve all your problems by running away from them. Who says California is so great, anyway? People have been mining for gold there for years and I never heard of anyone striking it so rich they were able to just start their lives over."

He shrugged in that self-assured way he had and ran a hand through his brown hair. The sunlight painted it with flecks of gold, and I saw then that he was a beautiful man, much changed from the boy I had met only a few years before.

Could I love him? I wondered. My life would certainly be easier if the man I married was my best friend. Things wouldn't have to change between us. The only difference in our friendship would be an official-looking piece of paper.

But that was a lie I told myself in order to make things easier, and love was not easy.

"So we would be the first ones to make it," he said with a sad little smile.

I shook my head and sighed. "I want to go to college, Ben. I can't leave New York. I can't leave my family."

After a moment he nodded and looked up at me, his eyes squinted against the glare of the sun. "Yeah," he said. "It was just a daydream, anyway."

But I could tell by the disappointed tone of his voice that it was much more than that.

****

The next fall, two days after I turned nineteen, I came down with a cold. At first, it was only a case of the sniffles accompanied by a little cough. I attributed it to the afternoon I had spent in the park on my birthday; it was a tradition of mine and Ben's to have lunch under a particular tree on our respective birthdays and I hadn't wanted to postpone it despite the unseasonable coldness of the day. Our traditions were unbreakable.

By the following week my little cold had developed into pneumonia. My father sent for Dr. Hutchins when my fever soared past 104 degrees and I began talking nonsense to anyone who would listen. The doctor advised Mother to keep me wrapped in a nightgown which had been soaked in cool water, but the heat from my body only absorbed the moisture and left the gown dry within an hour. I remember my sisters taking turns placing cool, wet cloths on my forehead and cheeks, and by then the fever was so intense I couldn't find the words to thank them. I barely had the strength to keep my eyes open, and what strength I did have was sapped by my coughing. Phlegm rattled in my chest like dry bones in a coffin.

I don't recall much of what happened over the next week. The fever ravaged my mind and body and all I could do was sleep and wish for death to embrace me. When I was awake it was difficult to ignore the worried glances my parents kept exchanging and the wordless melancholy that fell over my sisters. I think they were coming to terms with the fact that I would probably die.

I do remember a blur of visitors, family mostly, although my mother did allow Ben to come in and sit with me. At one point, he fed me small chips of ice with a spoon and I could only groan with pleasure at the moisture on my cracked lips.

I had never felt anything like that fever; I burned with it for five days and six nights and every hour was more excruciating than the last. My veins felt eaten up with dull fire, my blood like boiling lava. At one point I began to scream and was simply unable to stop, until at last my voice gave out and I collapsed in exhaustion.

Finally, on the sixth night, the medication Dr. Hutchins had given me began to work it's magic. My fever began to break, little by little, and at last I was able to take a deep breath that wasn't filled with pain. Finally, with only a bit of a wheeze to my breathing, I slept.

When I woke, I knew it was late by the darkness at my window. The house was quiet but for the ticking of the clock on the mantle. I looked around my bedroom with a fresh perspective; this was the same room I had slept in for years, yet it looked different to me. The antique dollhouse my mother gave me for my sixth birthday sat on the hearth rug, the same as it had since I was a child, but it was changed, too. Where before it was a child's plaything, now it was a lovely piece of history. It slowly began to dawn on me that I really had been on the verge of death. Only such a close brush with the reaper could make old things seem new again.

"She lives," said a voice on my right, and I gasped and pulled the bedcovers up over myself. It was Ben, sitting in the rocking chair beside my bed with an afghan over his legs.

"What are you doing here?" I croaked. "It's late."

"Do you really think I would leave you here in the care of your family? Your mother can barely keep her rosebushes alive."

I managed a laugh, or what passed for one, and sat up with a bit of difficulty. Ben was immediately at my side, his warm hand at my elbow. I felt him place an extra pillow behind my head and leaned back, grateful he was there. My body was still incredibly weak, my legs like thin sticks beneath the blankets. I couldn't remember eating anything while the fever ravaged my body and said as much to Ben.

"We took turns feeding you broth," he said, and pushed my

hair back from my forehead. "But mostly what you wanted was ice."

"*We?*" I repeated. "How long have you been here?"

"The whole time," he said with a little smile. "Even saw a bit of you naked when your mother was bathing you."

I swatted him weakly and laughed, a laugh which quickly turned into a cough. It seemed I wasn't entirely out of the woods.

"Bite your tongue! You did no such thing," I said.

He handed me a glass of cool water from the pitcher on my nightstand and sat beside me as I nursed it. When I handed it back to him, the glass was almost empty and my throat felt soothed, as though the water had coated it.

"I've been taking turns with your family to watch over you. Your mother just went to bed a little while ago. Poor kid. She's exhausted."

I leaned back against the pillows and tried to remember what day I had originally fallen ill. It seemed like only a couple of days had passed, but when I recalled my scattered memories during the time of my fever, it became clear that I had been in bed much longer than that.

"Nine days," Ben said when I asked for an answer. "Longest nine days of my entire life. I...I was really scared, Lucy," he said quietly. All signs of playfulness were gone from his face. "I started thinking about what I would do if I lost you."

I looked up at him and gave what I hoped was a reassuring smile. "But you didn't. You're not going to get rid of me that easily."

Instead of retorting, he leaned down slowly, until his mouth was a bare breath from mine, and hovered there for a moment. I felt paralyzed. I couldn't move my face away from his. I could only look into his eyes and wait for the inevitable kiss...

But it never came. He moved his cheek against mine instead and pressed his lips to my jaw, and then pulled away again.

I felt my eyes begin to well up and turned away so he

wouldn't mistake my tears for something they weren't. I was so overwhelmed with gratitude for my friend, this man who loved me enough to stay with me through a terrifying illness and watch as my family prepared themselves for my death. That alone would have been enough to bring tears to my eyes, but I was crying because his feelings for me were so obvious and I knew it was causing him pain to continue a friendship with me when there was no promise of a romance.

"I know you love me the best you can," he said suddenly, and I turned to him, unmindful of the tears. It was as though he had read my mind. "I'll have to be happy with that."

When I couldn't find words, he leaned in close and kissed me on the forehead, the way my father sometimes did.

"I would rather have you as my best friend than not at all, Lucinda."

I let him wrap his arms around me then, and after a moment I put mine around his neck, and he held me that way for some time. He smelled good, like soap and tobacco. There was nothing I could say that would ease the awkwardness of the moment, and so I said nothing. But after a while, I longed to hear his voice again. The silence in the room was filled with tension.

"Tell me the story of Castor and Pollux," I said finally. The words came out muffled against his neck.

Instead of teasing me for requesting to hear a myth he himself had told me a hundred times, he smiled and brought his hand up to stroke my hair. After a few moments, he began.

"Castor and Pollux were twins, the sons of Leda and Zeus. Well, they shared the same mother but had different fathers, which meant that Pollux was immortal and Castor was mortal...and I guess that also means they weren't really twins, but Greek mythology doesn't care much about small matters like that. Anyway, when Castor died, Pollux asked Zeus to let him share his own immortality with his brother to keep them together, and they were transformed into the Gemini constellation..."

Chapter Two

After I began to build my strength back up and Dr. Hutchins declared that I was going to be alright, things went back to normal in our house. My mother brought me toast and tea one morning and sat with me for some time, telling me about the new charity organization she had founded with her good friend Eleanor Buckman--a hospital for animals--and that my father had just taken on a huge case that kept him in Boston for several days at a time. It was easy, light conversation and I enjoyed it very much, as before my illness I had never had much time alone with my mother. But inevitably, our conversation soon turned to more serious matters.

"I can't believe how much better you look," she said, brushing back my hair as she had done when I was young. She took my hands in hers for a moment. "I hate to think about how fragile you were just a few days ago. I was so scared for you, Lucinda."

"I had so many people taking good care of me it would have been nearly impossible for me not to get better," I said. "I only wish I had been in my right mind the last time Dr. Hutchins was here so I could have thanked him."

"I believe your father showed the good doctor enough gratitude for all of us," Mother said with a smile. "These past few days, I have seen your father get down on his knees and pray more than I have during the course of our entire marriage. As soon as you started to beat your fever, he invited the doctor over for Christmas dinner!"

"I'm sorry I scared everyone," I said. "I'm a lucky girl to have so many people care about me,"

"Well, your father had to leave again this morning, but he said to tell you he loves you and that as soon as you feel up to it he wants to take you out. If I were you, I'd push for a shopping trip. He might just feel obliged to buy you a whole new wardrobe."

I laughed and took her hand. "Thank you, Mother. For

everything you've done."

She leaned forward and kissed my nose and I was enveloped in her scent, a mixture of rosewater and Ivory soap.

"I didn't do anything but love you, darling. That's what us mothers do."

A moment later she left me to get my rest, and I dreamt of the way her cool, soft hands had felt on mine and of the way she smelled. It was a memory I would cherish for some time.

****

Later, I decided to spend some time with my sisters, who had nursed me so lovingly when I was in the throes of my illness. That night as a thunderstorm raged outside, I invited them into my room for cookies and milk and scary stories, just as I had when we were children. We sat in a circle on my bed and told tall tales of headless horsemen and ghostly ladies who haunted their unfaithful husbands.

Soon, though, our talk turned to silly things, like how Andrew Watkins had fallen off the ladder in the library after Elizabeth walked by in her new dress.

'I think I'll wear that dress to the library every time I go from now on," she said with a mischievous little smile, and Emily and I giggled. Elizabeth had entertained a crush on Andrew since she was twelve years old.

"I want to know who you fancy, Lucy," Emily said, poking me lightly in the ribs.

"Yes, there must be someone good enough for you to marry," Elizabeth said with a little smile.

I lowered my head. "There isn't anyone yet."

"But surely you do *think* about it," Emily persisted. "For goodness' sake, it's all I can do to think about anything else! In fact, I've been keeping a scrapbook of pictures I've cut out of magazines, photos of wedding dresses and the sort of flowers I want...by the time someone proposes to me I'll have the entire thing planned out!"

I smiled and shook my head. That was such an Emily thing

to do, I thought. She had always been the one to plan out our day when we were younger, the organized one who kept lists and journals for everything.

"Of course I think about it," I said. I looked over Emily's head, out the window to the storm that walked and talked outside, and thought back to when Ben had come so close to kissing me. Was I being cruel and selfish to deny something that could be wonderful? Was it just the fear of losing his friendship that kept me from letting myself love him, or something else? My head hurt with the questions.

"I think about it," I repeated, "But I also think about going to college and traveling. We are extraordinarily lucky girls, do you realize that? We have the means to do anything we want to do. Most people don't have that luxury right now."

Elizabeth flopped back on the bed and made an exasperated sound. "College? Pshh. School is boring! We're young, we should be courting and going to fashion shows and enjoying the city! Not sticking ourselves in a classroom for hours at a time."

"I just don't think we should limit ourselves, that's all," I said quietly. "Besides, there isn't even anyone interested in me. You can't get married without a man."

"What about Ben?" Emily asked softly, and I turned to look at her, to see if she was teasing me, but her expression was serious.

"Ben is my best friend. I don't think about him that way."

Emily picked up the empty milk pitcher and stood from the bed. "He stayed here for over a week when you were sick. He slept on that lumpy couch in the parlor and didn't go to work, hardly ate anything, and nursed you when we couldn't. That sounds like more than just a friend, Luce."

With that, she turned to make her way to the kitchen to refill the pitcher, and I was left with a curious look from Elizabeth and the sound of the leaves shaking off beads of rain outside the window.

****

The next day I gathered up what little energy I had, bundled up in the new wool-lined coat my father had given me for my birthday and walked over to Ben's house. I had been stuck inside for weeks, first battling my illness and then recovering from it, and I had more than a small case of cabin fever. Besides, I had a new dress that had never seen the light of day, a gorgeous peacock blue with green edging, and I wanted to show it off.

The leaves had changed their color already, turning the trees along the street into matches that had been struck alight. Somewhere close, someone was making apple cider. I breathed in deep and then doubled over in a coughing fit that made my lungs feel like an accordion that had been pressed together. I heard a loose rattling in my chest and knew I still had a bit to go in the last stage of my recovery.

Looking back, I should have turned around right then and gone straight to bed. But I was so sick of being trapped inside, and the leaves were gorgeous even in their death throes, and the day was mine to do as I pleased; and so I continued up the steps in front of Ben's townhouse and tried not to breathe too deeply, for fear it would bring on another round of coughing.

"Lucy! What are you doing here? You should be resting!" Ben exclaimed when he opened the door. He reached for me immediately and pulled me inside, rubbing his hands along my arms as though I had been shivering and needed body heat.

"I'm fine!" I assured him. "I had to get out of the house, the silence is driving me mad."

"Where is everyone?"

"Elizabeth and Emily went to a tea social, my mother is meeting with an architect she hired to build the new animal hospital, and Father is still in Boston."

"Why didn't you just call me? I would have come to you."

"That's just the point, dear Ben," I said, poking him in the chest. "I can't stand being stuck in that house one more minute, alone or otherwise. I want to go to a movie."

He searched my eyes then, looking for some sign that I was too unwell to go, I suppose. After a moment, he must have liked what he saw, because he grabbed his coat from a hook on the wall behind him and took my hand.

"If it's a movie the lady wants, a movie she shall have," he said, and opened the door for me with a little bow.

I laughed. "Why, thank you," I said. "You certainly are a gentleman after I have a brush with death. Maybe I should have them more often."

I made my way carefully down the front steps and turned when I realized he wasn't at my side. He stood at the front door, looking down at me with a bizarre mixture of anger and sadness on his face.

"For Heaven's sake, Ben, what's the matter?"

"Don't tease me about that, Lucy. It's not funny."

I lowered my head, instantly regretful of my careless words. I had meant it to sound playful and had wound up hurting him instead.

"I'm sorry, Ben," I said softly. "I wasn't thinking. Of course it isn't funny. And I can't begin to tell you how much I appreciate that you were there with me. I don't think I would have made it without you."

He walked slowly down the steps until he was standing on the one above me and took my hands in his.

"I don't think you understand how much you mean to me, Lucy. Even if you don't..." He trailed off then, seemed to rethink his words, and then continued with a thoughtful look on his face. "Even if you *can't* love me, you are still the person who matters most to me in the world."

"Oh, Ben, I do love you--"

He shook his head. "Not the way I need you to. And that's alright, really. I understand. But I will always make you my highest priority. I will always take care of you. We're like Castor and Pollux, remember?"

I smiled and nodded, feeling my eyes prickle. "Thank you. For everything."

He inclined his head and squeezed my hands. "Let's go see a picture show, what do you say?"

"I say okay."

He led me down the steps then and we walked the ten blocks to the Imperial Theater. He held my hand the entire way.

****

The Imperial was a lovely theater with gilded woodwork and red velvet tapestries hanging everywhere. It had been one of my favorite places in New York for several years, ever since Father took me to see *The Love Parade* when I was fourteen. That was in '29, and films had come a long way from even the year before, when silent stars ruled the big screen.

I'll never forget that day with Father; as soon as I took my seat in that cushioned chair my world changed for the better. I had never imagined such beauty and magical ambiance as that which emanated from the projector. During the entire length of the movie, I sat on the edge of the seat with my elbows resting on my knees. I don't even believe I blinked, I was so transfixed. I suddenly wished I was up there with those gorgeous young ingenues, speaking with such emotion and self-confidence.

Arm in arm with Ben, I told him as much as we walked through the theater lobby. He laughed and shook his head.

"I will never understand why girls feel the need to compare themselves to the rich and famous. You are ten times more beautiful than any of those actresses. And I'm willing to bet you have more personality in your little finger than they do, too."

I felt my cheeks get hot and gave a little laugh of my own. "You sure know how to give a girl a compliment, don't you?"

"Aww, come on Luce, don't be such a girl. You know how gorgeous you are. And if you don't, then I guess I'm doing something wrong."

I wondered what exactly he saw when he looked at me....if he saw a beautiful girl, or just a girl whose insides were beautiful. I had never thought of myself as anything but a fair girl with dark, curly hair and blue eyes. My mother used to say I looked like a porcelain doll, but where she saw beauty I only

16

saw plainness.

Just then, the big clock in the lobby struck one, signaling the start of the movie. A queue began forming at the ticket taker's booth and we wandered over to join the line. As we did so, Ben's words echoed in my brain; he thought I was gorgeous. I was rendered speechless....and also a little guilty. And with that pang of guilt came something else: anger. He knew how I felt; why couldn't he keep comments like that to himself? They only served to make me uncomfortable.

I came very close to saying something to him about it, but then I glanced at him and saw how happy he was in that moment, with my arm laced through his and the promise of a lovely day ahead. He didn't ask for much, I thought. He had stayed with me while I was ill and had taken care of me, and the only thing he requested in return was something I was already giving him: my friendship.

The angry words died on my lips. I couldn't do that to him.

"Ready?" he asked, staring at me. We had advanced in line and he had already given our tickets to the man at the booth, who was looking at me curiously. It occurred to me that I had probably been standing there with an odd mixture of exasperation, anger, and love on my face and I quickly smiled to cover it.

"Ready as I'll ever be."

He smiled and escorted me into the theater, and as we walked I suppressed a tickle in my chest that wanted to become a cough.

****

The movie that day was *Happiness Ahead,* and I enjoyed it immensely from the beginning. After a little while, I could feel Ben starting to squirm in his seat as though he was uncomfortable and I asked him if he wanted to go, but he simply smiled and shook his head. I didn't think much about it at the time, but now I believe that if his chair had been filled with pins and needles, he would have sat there just as still as a statue if he thought staying would make me happy.

About an hour into the movie, my chest began to feel tight. I sat up straighter, hoping to relieve some of the pressure on my lungs, but to no avail. It was that pressed accordion feeling again, and it frightened me. I retrieved a handkerchief from my purse and coughed into it as lightly as I could, hoping it wouldn't trigger an uncontrollable fit.

"Are you alright?" Ben whispered, leaning in close to my ear.

"I'm fine," I said, and forced a smile.

The truth was, I wasn't fine. It was becoming harder to breathe by the second. My windpipe felt as though a large hand was wrapped around it, slowly increasing pressure. I coughed again, and this time I heard the old familiar rattle of phlegm in my chest.

What I didn't know was that my lungs had slowly filled with fluid when I had pneumonia and was the cause of most of the weakness and fatigue I had felt over the past weeks. I don't believe there was anything that could have been done if I *had* known; I think it was too late by that point. At least, that's what I tell myself.

"Would you like me to get you some water?" Ben asked, and I could see the worried expression on his face even in the semi-darkness. The screen threw squares of white and grey light onto his face, making me think of the shadow a tree throws onto a sidewalk.

"That would be nice," I said, trying unsuccessfully not to croak the words.

He jumped up at once and edged his way past me to get to the aisle. I noticed a few people who had turned around in their seats to see what was going on and tried to look inconspicuous. I managed to hold off on another cough for a couple of minutes, but by the time Ben returned with a small cup of water I was almost retching into my handkerchief. Someone opened the theater door--an usher, I suppose--and said, "Does she need help?"

I was fighting for every breath, close to hyperventilation,

18

and could barely concentrate on what was going on around me, but I got the sense that most people had stopped paying attention to the movie entirely to gather round the group of seats where we were.

"My God, Luce, you're bleeding!" Ben cried suddenly, and somewhere in the crowd a lady gasped. I brought my fingers up to my mouth and they came away slick with blood.

"We've got to get you to the hospital," he said, and began to lift me out of my seat. The movement compressed my lungs and I cried out, suddenly more scared than I had ever been in my life. The sight of one's own blood has that effect, I suppose, especially in such a happy place as a theater. It seemed so out of place, as though juxtaposed from someone else's life perhaps.

Ben knelt on the floor in front of me and held my face gently. He spoke softly and calmly, but I knew that inside he was screaming. He told me I had to stand up and walk with him. He would get me to the hospital, he said, but first I had to find the strength to stand, because he couldn't lift me without hurting me. Could I do that? He asked.

And just when I thought I could possibly do as he asked, that the coughing fit had subsided for a moment, another wave hit me and I doubled over. A thick glob of mucus came up and I gagged, trying to expel it, but it was almost spongy and refused to move. I looked around wildly at the faces above me, pale ovals in the dim light, and had a very clear thought: I was going to die in this theater. I was going to die in front of Ben and a group of people I didn't even know. I was going to leave my sisters behind and my parents brokenhearted.

Dimly, I heard Ben screaming for help as he realized what was happening. I heard the panicked cries of others in the room who knew that I was choking to death and couldn't do a thing for me. I felt Ben's cool hand on my warm one, squeezing, and then he hauled me out of my seat and began beating me on the back in an effort to knock the phlegm out of my throat.

Then, as slowly as water swirling down a drain, I began to lose consciousness. I heard the noises of the theater in echo, as though I was standing at the end of a long tunnel. I saw bright flashes of light that I knew to be the projector, still whirring behind us because the person running it wasn't aware of what was happening. I felt Ben's strong hand on my back and wished I could tell him not to be scared. Things weren't so bad; I actually started to feel a bit better as I drooped forward, losing strength in my legs. My lungs had lost that tight feeling. I began to feel so tired, so extraordinarily sleepy...

And then, as a group of strangers and the man who loved me looked on, I felt nothing at all.

Chapter Three

For a while after that day, I wasn't completely sure of what had happened. I wandered down a long, twisty corridor for what seemed like a very long time. The walls on either side of me were painted deep crimson and were decorated with photographs of my family and friends in ornate, gilded frames. I came across several that depicted moments in my life which had been forgotten, days and events that hadn't crossed my mind in years. Some were so old I had no recollection of them at all, such as the day I was born and the night Emily, who was two years older than me, came into the world.

I had time to wonder who had taken these photos and where I was, exactly, but there were no answers forthcoming. I was completely alone. I discovered that although I was confused and more than a bit lonely, I wasn't scared, and that was a relief. I had the distinct feeling that wherever I had been previous to this was a frightening place. Odd, disjointed memories floated up to the surface of my brain: pale faces staring down at me in a darkened room, someone hitting me hard across the back, the feeling that I couldn't catch my breath. And always, no matter what the memory was, the sensation that I was forgetting something followed it. Something important.

I never knew how long I stayed in that meandering hallway, journeying past a photographic chronicle of my life as that nagging feeling of something lost plagued me. It might have been hours or days. Weeks or months. Years or decades. Time didn't seem to mean much there. And when I did at last come to a door, it seemed I had only been walking for a few moments.

It was large, that door, and the knob was brass and scrolled with some sort of ancient writing I didn't understand. I grasped it boldly, glad to finally have an end to my journey, and right before I opened the door I had time to think that perhaps I was wrong; perhaps the journey was just starting.

As soon as I stepped through to the other side, a wave of memories hit me and I actually stumbled back with the weight of them, grasping the doorframe to regain my balance. What stood before me was perplexing, familiar, and altogether horrifying.

The Imperial Theater, in all its glory, was waiting for me.

****

The room was cool and dark and silent. I stood still for a moment, reliving the events that had taken place not more than twelve feet from where I stood. I could almost see Ben's sweet face in the darkness, could almost hear the gasps of the ladies who had witnessed my death. But as real as the memories were, they were just that: memories. I was alone in the theater with only my thoughts to keep me company.

Looking back on it, I suppose it's odd that I never even considered the possibility that I was dreaming, or had gone crazy, or both. But being forced back into that theater, reliving the moments of my own death, was the harshest reality I had ever endured. I don't believe I could have convinced myself it was a dream even if I'd wanted to. In my first moments back, I made myself accept what I knew to be true. It was the pragmatist I had been in life roaring back to full, pulsing vitality, pushing me to deal with what was before me in whatever way I was able. Perhaps it was also my way of grasping something from my old life, something familiar and ingrained so deeply in my personality that it could not be ignored. It was much like a slap in the face, or a dash of cold water to wake a person up. And inside, I heard my mother's voice, guiding me towards the stronger path despite the pain it held. She had always been strong, my mother. She would not tolerate anything less in her daughters.

After what seemed like a very long time, I forced my legs to move and sat down in one of the seats after glancing over my shoulder at the door. Where it had been, there was now only a solid wall.

Again, time did that strange little dance with me. I have no idea how long I sat there, thinking of my family and asking myself endless questions which I knew would never be answered. The only thing I knew for sure was that I was scared to leave that theater (*could* I leave, I wondered?), terrified of what waited for me out in the world. Was there even a world there? Did reality exist for me in this state? Could I haunt people?

At some point, I slept. Or maybe I just fell into a state of repose and sat in a trance-like stupor. I managed to turn my brain off for a while, and that was what really mattered. I was suddenly so very tired, and that reminded me of my last living days. I wanted, more than anything else, to rest.

Finally, after what seemed like a lifetime of sitting in solitude, something happened. The big double doors which opened into the theater were pulled apart and a shaft of light split the darkness in half. I squinted at the sudden brightness and shielded my eyes to try and see who had just come in, but they were just vague shadows upon shadows. I got the impression that several people had streamed in and yet I couldn't make out individuals at all, only irregular shaped masses. It took a moment for my mind to comprehend what I was seeing, and when it did my mouth fell open in awe.

They *were* people, of that I was sure, but they weren't fully formed into human shapes; the things that floated all around me were made of a black smoke-like substance. They blurred into one another, moving quickly around the room, and even as I watched they began to take on a more substantial form, changing from smoke and shadows to skin and bone. Before five minutes had passed, I was sitting in a room filled with perhaps a hundred people, all of them talking and laughing and filled with life. The overhead lights had come on too, I realized; I had been so engrossed in watching the newcomers that I hadn't even noticed. As I sat there among those people, listening to their excited conversation and feeling the buzz of life all around me, I felt tears well up in my eyes. Those tears were for my mother and father, for my sisters, for Ben...and a little for myself. But they were also for the realization that had hit me: I had just witnessed a moment in time come into being.

****

I sat for hours, watching the people around me and observing details about their dress, their hairstyles, and their manner of speaking. It seemed that most of those things hadn't changed much and I concluded that I couldn't have been gone very long. The movie that was playing was one I had never heard of, however.

No one seemed to notice me, yet I realized after a while that not one person had tried to sit in my seat. I wondered if they felt a wave of coldness emanating from it and steered clear automatically, or if perhaps it was just blind luck.

I began to try to work up the courage to leave the theater. *What's the worst that could happen?* I asked myself. *You're already dead.* The words echoed in my mind. Despite what I knew and what my own eyes told me, I found it difficult to come to terms with the fact that I had passed over into some realm between the living and the dead. I felt a great sadness wash over me, but I was unable to cry. I wanted to; I felt I would begin to accept what had happened if I could. But I couldn't do it. I felt numb.

Just as I was telling myself for the third time to get up and walk to the doors, a young man came strolling down the aisle and sat in the seat beside me. I watched him carefully to see if he gave any sign that he was aware of my presence, and for a moment he simply watched the screen. But then, to my great surprise, he turned to me.

"Hello," he said with a smile. "You're new here, aren't you?"

I opened my mouth to speak and nothing came out.

"I know, it's a bit of a shock at first, isn't it? Watching time start up in front of your eyes, seeing all these living people going about their business and completely ignoring you, and all the while you're wondering about the family you left behind and whether you can travel outside this room. Someone should

24

really create a handbook for the new arrivals."

"That was real, then? The smoke-people?" I whispered, leaning in toward him eagerly.

"Oh it was real, alright," he said, and ran a hand through his dark hair. He was handsome in an unconventional way--his nose had been broken at some point and had never quite healed correctly--and spoke with a vague Irish accent. "What you witnessed was the great wheel of life spinning into motion. No one understands it, not really, but my theory is that things are sort of paused for us until we come out of that corridor and become acclimated to our new...ah....situation...and then, after a while, things start up again."

"You've been in the corridor?" I laid my hand on his arm, excited to have found someone who knew what I had been through, and discovered the oddest thing: touching him was like touching the surface of a soap bubble. He felt delicate and insubstantial, as though one wrong move would damage him.

He nodded. "We all go through it, only it's different for each person."

"What do you mean?"

"Well, from what I can gather, most of us see photos of our family and friends, the people we left behind. There are images that capture moments in our lives that stand out to us, such as birthdays and holidays and the like, and then there are pictures of events we don't even remember. For me it was the funeral of my father, who died a month before I was born."

I nodded excitedly. "Yes, I had photographs like those in my corridor! There was one of my sister on the night she was born, and she is--was--two years older than me. I didn't understand why it was with the others."

"No one knows why," he said, shaking his head. "But I have heard tales of those who see much different images in their corridors. Murderers and thieves, mostly...evil people. Word is, they are surrounded by pictures of their own wrongdoings, as well as the aftermath. And they don't eventually come to a door, like we did. They just have to walk the length of that hallway forever, surrounded by photographic

25

evidence of their guilt."

I sat back and let that sink in. If what he said was true, did that mean the corridor was some sort of limbo? Or was it simply a path for some and Hell for others?

"I know it's all confusing," he said, watching me. "You'll get used to things soon enough. We all do what we can to adjust."

"Yes, I suppose so," I said. "May I ask you something?"

"Anything at all, pretty lady."

"How did you know I was...you know...."

"A ghost?"

"Yes. A ghost." Saying the word aloud sent gooseflesh racing up my back.

"From your aura. It's brighter than any I've ever seen, and rainbow colored. I spotted it even in the dark. Beautiful."

"My aura?" I repeated.

"It's sort of a glow that hangs around your head. You'll notice them soon enough. That's how we find one another, how we differentiate between the living and the dead."

"So we can travel? What I mean to say is, I'm not stuck here?"

"Heavens no! You can go just about anywhere you please. You must have..." He trailed off, looking at me intently in the glow of the movie screen. "You died here, didn't you?"

I lowered my head. "Yes. Is that why I was returned here?"

"I believe so. I think that happens to all of us. Perhaps it's a way to get us to remember what happened so we don't walk around thinking we're still alive, like poor Albert."

"Albert?"

He smiled and shook his head. "Not important. Just someone I met a long time ago."

"Oh." I faced forward and looked at the screen, at Ginger Rogers and Fred Astaire gliding across a dancefloor, and let my mind race. I felt better than I had since I was sent back to the theater; now I had a few answers, a new friend, and a goal. I had to find Ben.

"Listen, I'd better be going. I just stopped in to see Ginger."

He gestured to the movie screen. "She's as beautiful as ever."

"Well, I'm awfully glad you did. Thank you so much, really. I feel a lot better."

He grinned, and I could see that he probably had his choice of the ladies when he was alive. That smile was endearing.

"Not a problem at all, Miss...?"

"Lucy," I said, holding out my hand. "Lucy Garside."

"Pleasure to meet you, Miss Lucy Garside," he said, and stood up, taking my hand and giving a little bow. "You can call me Irish."

Just then, the house lights came up and I squinted automatically, then realized it wasn't necessary. Apparently when you're a ghost, bright light doesn't bother you. I looked up at Irish and saw the most wonderous thing: his aura. It was a deep turquoise blue, the color of the ocean, and undulated in waves around his head. It was gorgeous.

"I'll see you around, Miss Lucy," he said, and turned to leave.

"Wait! Irish!"

He looked back at me over his shoulder and I stood up, unmindful of the people streaming around us toward the double doors.

"Is it God who sent us here? Have you seen Him?"

He laughed good-naturedly and shook his head. "That I don't know, Miss Lucy. But if I ever run into him I'll let you know."

And with that, he was gone, and I was left alone to face a new world.

Chapter Four

My first hours outside the theater were confusing ones. I walked the city streets, observing everything, trying to ascertain exactly how long I had been gone, but for the most part things remained unchanged from when I'd left. Even the trees looked the same. At that point I realized I was wearing the same lovely blue dress I had died in, yet I wasn't cold, even though my new wool coat hadn't made the trip with me. I remembered that I had taken it off in the theater before the movie started. I wondered if Ben had given it back to my parents.

Poor Ben, I thought with an inward groan. He had been forced to watch me choke to death, had even tried to help me at the end. I wished I'd gotten to say goodbye. I wanted to see him so badly, yet I didn't dare go to his house. I told myself it was because part of me was afraid that he would somehow see me and the shock of it would cause him to have a heart attack, but another part of me, a bigger part, knew it was because I didn't want to see him in mourning. I had hurt him enough while I was alive; I was loathe to see what state he would be in after witnessing my death.

Day was turning into night as I walked, yet I still had no destination in mind. I longed to step foot inside my house again, to see my family and smell the familiar scents of our kitchen: banana nut bread, cinnamon, apples, coffee. I wanted more than anything to hear my sisters bickering over some inane thing, but I was scared of what I would find if I went there so I walked instead. I made my way to Central Park and sat beneath the tree that Ben and I had declared "ours". Dusk was falling rapidly and hardly a soul walked about the paths. I found I could barely feel the grass beneath me and recalled the delicate nature of Irish's skin, how he had felt insubstantial. It made me wonder what it would be like to have a human touch me.

Finally, I dug up the courage to venture to my house. I

assured myself that I could simply walk by if I wanted, perhaps look into the windows and peek in on my family, but in my heart I knew I wouldn't be able to resist going in. I was a mess that night, completely alone and terrified of my strange new world, and I couldn't imagine a more welcome sight than my old rambling townhouse. I was only hesitant to go there because I had a feeling I would find my sisters grief-stricken, my parents in shock. It would break my heart to see them that way.

I walked slowly, savoring the scents of fall in the city. A fine mist had begun to creep up, lending a soft glow to the streetlamps above me. It all made me want to wrap my arms around myself and suddenly I appreciated my immunity to the cold.

When I made it home at last, I found myself in a bit of a quandary: I wasn't entirely sure how to get inside. When I'd left the theater I had simply walked out amidst the stream of people flowing out the front doors, careful not to bump into an elbow or step on anyone's toes. That was an impossibility here, unless someone opened the door from the other side to leave, allowing me to quickly slip in. As it was fairly late at night, I figured the odds of that happening were slim to none. I was just about to content myself with looking in through the front window when a sudden inspiration hit me. I climbed up the front steps and stood before the door, concentrating on it as hard as I could. I imagined myself moving through it, as easily as a bubble moves through the air, and in the next moment I was on the other side.

I smiled and inwardly congratulated myself on figuring out an essential bit of ghostly knowledge. *Irish would be proud*, I thought. And then I brought all my attention to my surroundings.

The house smelled the same. It crossed my mind to wonder how I could detect scents if I wasn't breathing, but then I realized I *was* breathing; shallowly and slowly, although the effects weren't the same as when I was alive. I didn't actually need to breathe, I simply did it because I always had. But I pushed those thoughts away; the enormity of being back home was more important. I could hear small things rustling behind the baseboards in the foyer and imagined mice scurrying back home after sensing an unfamiliar presence. To my right was the staircase, and at the top of it were two rooms, belonging to my sisters. I heard someone speaking up there in a low voice, but not clearly enough to hear what they were saying. The parlor was empty and I could see, from my position in the hallway, that there was no one in the kitchen.

I glanced up the stairs, gathering the strength to go up. If I'd had a working heart, I imagine it would have been pounding at that point. My excitement at seeing my sisters again was so great it almost drowned out the anxious little voice in my head that told me I was about to walk into something bad, something I didn't want to see. *Almost.*

I glided up and paused at the landing, trying to ascertain which door the voices were behind. They seemed to be coming from Emily's room, so I moved in that direction and saw immediately that the door was cracked open a bit. Not knowing for sure if I could send myself through a door that wasn't fully closed, I settled instead for leaning down and peering through the opening.

"I haven't cried so much in my whole life," Emily was saying. Her voice sounded thick, as though she was crying at that very moment, and the sight of her shocked me. She was so thin, thinner than I had ever seen her, and her hair was in a tangle atop her head. Her eyes were reddened and puffy, which was understandable, but her appearance in general was heartbreaking. I could see the small knob of the top of her spine just above the back of her nightdress, which hung loosely on her.

"I haven't, either," an unfamiliar voice said. I craned my neck to see further into the room and caught a rather confusing glimpse of someone I hadn't expected to see: Mrs. Delacorte, Ben's mother. "It seems so cruel for such a young light to be extinguished."

The room was silent for a moment except for the sound of

an occasional sniffle.

"You should speak with Mother," Emily said finally. "She's refused to come out of her bedroom since it happened."

"I don't know that she's ready for visitors, Emily. I'm only here tonight because I saw your light on from across the way. Sleep hasn't been coming easily for you either, I take it?"

Emily shook her head. "Every time I close my eyes I see her face. When I am able to sleep, I dream of her. It's always the same...I see her as she looked on that day, beautiful and rested, but instead of only calling goodbye to her over my shoulder as I really did, I hug her and tell her I love her." Her voice cracked then and she bent over at the waist, too overcome with emotion to continue, and Mrs. Delacorte was at her side immediately with a comforting arm around her shoulders.

"She knew how much you loved her," Mrs. Delacorte said, pressing a handkerchief to her own eyes. "Don't tax yourself so, Emily, it isn't healthy. Lucy wouldn't want you to be so hard on yourself."

"Listen to me, prattling on about my own feelings while you're in mourning, too," Emily sniffled, wiping her eyes. "I'm sorry."

Mrs. Delacorte rubbed Emily's back in small, comforting circles and brought the handkerchief to her eyes again, and all the while I wondered, *Who is she in mourning for? Me?*

It wasn't entirely out of the realm of possibility, I supposed, but it was a bit strange. Although Ben and I had been as close as brother and sister, I hadn't known his mother very well, She was nice enough when I visited, but I always got the feeling from her that I was wasting Ben's time, time he could have been using to find a suitable wife.

"I just miss him so much," Mrs. Delacorte said, her words bringing on a fresh bout of tears.

HIM?

I staggered back, bringing my hand to my mouth as I did. It couldn't be. No, it couldn't be what I thought....

"I knew he loved Lucy, but to take his own life....I'm so afraid for his soul," Mrs. Delacorte said, the last word turning

31

into a sob, and as she finally broke down in my sister's arms I fled down the staircase, not even pausing at the front door. In a moment I was through it and the night sky was above me, and under the watchful eyes of Castor and Pollux I lifted my head and screamed toward the heavens.

****

Time. Someone somewhere once called it the "old bald cheater", and I believe that's as good a description as any. It gives, and then it takes away. It moves with agonizing slowness when what you want the most is for it to hurry along, and speeds up just when things are going well.

In my world, time doesn't mean much. A year can feel like a few minutes, an hour like a handful of weeks. I came to be very grateful for the Imperial Theater, because as the years went by it was my haven, the place I felt safe in a crowded world, and it was at once a refuge and a measurement of time. I was able to keep up with trends, fashions, the gradual change in language and attitude. I listened to the people around me to glean information that movies couldn't or wouldn't give. I listened, and I watched. By 1989 I felt the way a person who has lived to be a hundred must feel, yet I was stuck in the body of a nineteen year old girl. I had witnessed a lifetime of history through film and the music that accompanied it.

There were times, back in the old days, when I visited my family. I wasn't strong enough to stay away, even after the night I learned Ben had killed himself. I used to sneak in at night and listen to my sisters' conversations and smile as they reminisced about me and our childhoods. They spoke about me almost as though I had only gone away to college instead of choking to death in a theater, and I realized that was their way of dealing with my leaving them; I noticed they never used the word "dead".

My mother died of a stroke in 1947. For a while after my death, she was inconsolable and stayed in her room for weeks, refusing to eat much more than toast with her morning tea.

32

After about two months, though, she came back to her old self. It was the charities that did it; she got word that the animal hospital was falling apart at the seams and decided to jump back into her old schedule in order to make things run more smoothly. In the end I believe that's what did her in; she took too much onto herself and was too stubborn to say no to anyone who asked for her help. The woman who wouldn't let labor pains stop her from taking a walk in the park was certainly not going to let a busy schedule get in the way of her charity work.

My father died soon thereafter. The doctor pronounced the cause of death a heart attack, but I think it was simply broken. My mother was his world, had been since the day they met, and when she died he just didn't know what to do with himself.

By that time, both my sisters were married and had moved on, Emily to Boston and Elizabeth to Vermont. When they came home for the funeral they stood in the parlor together and looked around at the house they had grown up in. I'm sure it seemed small to them, the same but different; much the way my room had looked to me the day I woke up after beating my fever. They never knew that as they stood on the large hooked rug my grandmother had made, I was beside them, wishing I could cry along with them, wishing I could hold their hands and tell them how proud I was of them and how much I loved them.

Before I left that day, I returned to my old room one last time and found my prized locket in the jewelry box on my bureau; I had forgotten to put it on the day Ben and I went to the theater. It was a lovely antique given to me by my father, passed down through our family for ages, and the brass was worn at the edges by years of being opened and closed again. I clicked open the scrolled lid and looked down at the faces inside; Elizabeth, Emily and I on the right and Ben on the left. I began to sob as I clasped it around my neck, knowing that everything had just been changed irrevocably and helpless to stop it. Life moved on without me.

I was always aware after that day that it was possible I would see my parents walking down the street at some point, hand in hand and with bright auras over their heads. I tried not to expect it and was unsuccessful; how could I not? I missed them so much and I had been alone for so long, and the idea of having them with me was too enticing to push out of my mind.

But I never saw them. I returned to our old townhouse even after another family moved in to see if I would find my father in his study, because he had died slumped over his desk. I visited the animal hospital (and spooked more than one cat) with the hope of catching my mother there. But they were never at either place, and after a while I gave up looking for them. I began to wonder if perhaps they had come to a different door at the end of their corridors, if they had perhaps gone somewhere completely unknown to me and the others walking around on Earth, but that only made me wonder why I had been chosen to stick around and so I usually pushed the thought away. Besides, thoughts of the corridor always made me remember what Irish had told me, about how it was different for everyone, which in turn made me think of Ben. I was scared to think of where he had gone.

*****

By the year 2008 I was fairly comfortable with the world I had created for myself. I had no possessions to cart around with me other than my journal, which doubled as a sketchbook. I had no need to eat, and finding shelter was easy, if not entirely necessary. I did still sleep every now and then, however; I suppose I was reluctant to give up every part of my old life, and besides, I found I became tired at times just like I had when I was alive. When those times came I would seek refuge at the Imperial or at the library, which had been one of my favorite places to go when I was alive. Both were also good places to people-watch, or to just sit and think. I did a lot of both over the years.

I also made a few friends of the ghostly variety. I saw quite a bit of my old pal Irish once I began to explore the city; he was a fixture at the New York City Library and when I ran into him there for the first time, I couldn't contain my surprise.

"What, did you think I spent all my time in pubs and back alleys?" he asked with the slightest hint of a grin.

"Of course not," I said, although I had envisioned exactly that upon our first meeting at the Imperial. "It's just that New York is such a large place that I never imagined I would see you again."

"Bad pennies have a way of turning up," he said, and gestured above our heads. "You'll find more of our kind upstairs, I suppose, if you feel like exploring. This place is sort of like a magnet, Miss Lucy. It draws us in after a while."

"And why is that?"

He shrugged and scratched the back of his head, mussing his hair in an endearing manner.

"I don't know for sure. I guess it's because when you have an eternity of time on your hands, you want to spend it doing something useful. Myself, I like to read Agatha Christie mysteries."

I smiled. "I never would have dreamed such a thing, Irish."

"It's our little secret," he said, putting a finger to his lips to mime that I should keep it quiet.

Indeed, I ran into several other ghosts at that library, but none who were as friendly as Irish. I learned to smile politely and keep moving when I saw another like myself, and that was something I didn't need to have explained to me; it was just common courtesy. We were all trying to figure out our paths in the afterlife and more than a few of us were mourning the loss of the people we had to leave behind. No one was there to make friends. We all just wanted to be left alone.

As much as I loved the hushed atmosphere of the library, I came to think of the Imperial as my home away from home. I realized how strange it was for me to form an attachment to the building I died in, but that in itself was part of the draw for me. As sad and frightening as my last moments were in the theater, they couldn't be overshadowed by the time I spent there with Ben, or the memories I had made there with my father. I traveled there often and enjoyed free movies and the company of fellow New Yorkers, who never knew they were sitting alongside a dead girl.

I probably saw upwards of a thousand films in that theater. Some were good, some were bad and some I can barely remember. But I will never, for as long as my spirit inhabits the Earth, forget the first time I saw Archer Black's face.

****

The film was titled "Crazy Love". I sat in the back of the theater and watched as a swarm of pre-teen girls filled the room, all giggly and whispery. Had I known about the reason for their manic happiness, I would have gotten pretty giggly myself, but I had never heard of this movie, and the stars were all relative unknowns in Hollywood.

The beginning credits were barely on the screen when a hush filled the room, pregnant with anticipation. I sat back in my seat, curiosity aroused, and watched as the most beautiful man I have ever seen appeared in full technicolor glory right in front of my eyes. I found I couldn't pay attention to the story that was unfolding; all I knew was the fullness of his lips, the unruly shock of dark hair that fell across his forehead, the way his dark--almost black--eyes seemed to pierce me from the screen.

I couldn't absorb the plot of the movie at all, and when he wasn't onscreen I began to get antsy in my seat, so strong was my desire to look at his face once more. He was almost ethereal, too beautiful to be true flesh and bone. *Who was this man*? I wondered. Was he even a man, or was he perhaps some sort of glorious creature created by a computer in order to attract hordes of screaming teenage girls?

He was real, alright. According to the conversations I casually eavesdropped on when the movie was over, his name was Archer Black and he split his time between Los Angeles and New York City.

"I heard he mostly stays in L.A. so he can be there for all the big celebrity events," I overheard one girl tell her friend.

Archer Black. What an absolutely thrilling name, I thought to myself when everyone had gone home for the night. The theater was mine again, dark and cool and silent. I was alone with my thoughts, my memories of his face and voice. I couldn't remember ever being so affected by someone I didn't know, or so attracted to a person's appearance. It was strange, the hold this man had on me. I daydreamed about him the way a girl with a schoolyard crush will do. I imagined meeting him, touching his strong hand, and the thought slammed a shot of reality into me that was as jarring as a bag of bricks falling on my head.

I was a ghost. We would never meet, he and I. I would never get to hear his voice say my name, and he would never know how he affected a girl who had been dead for seventy-five years. The realization saddened me beyond belief, and not just because I had forgotten my situation for a moment; it was also because, for the first time since I died, I was really lonely. Terribly, awfully lonely.

I thought of Ben and his sweet words the last time I saw him. It hurt my heart to think of him wandering down a lonesome corridor with no end in sight....if that was where he ended up. Right then, I would have given anything to see his face again. Anything at all.

****

On the night my sister Elizabeth died, a sudden storm blew in to the tiny town where she lived in Vermont. The wind gusted upwards of ninety miles an hour and pushed huge drifts of snow into the streets and on the sidewalks, barricading people in their homes. Icicles formed on eaves and tree limbs, catching the light to sparkle like diamonds. Elizabeth, who was by that time elderly and had been a widow for more than eight years, woke up briefly in the dark and saw the snow ticking at her window. She watched it for a moment, reminded of the first Christmas she spent with her husband and the romantic night they had spent together; the world had been suspended in a swirling white storm much like this one and they had shared a bottle of wine in bed, whispering and giggling like children. She thought of her son and daughter and of the family who had been called home before her: Mother, Father, and myself. And then, with the barest hint of a smile upon her lips, Elizabeth closed her eyes and let go.

I watched it all happen as I slept, and knew it was no ordinary dream when I woke up with tears in my eyes. I had just witnessed my sister passing on. I leaned forward in the theater seat I had fallen asleep in and covered my face with my hands, sobbing silently into them. How I missed my sisters! The years I'd spent without them, wandering the city on my own, had been almost colorless, devoid of the warmth my life had held.

"Miss Lucy?" a soft voice said at my side.

I looked up from my hands to see Irish standing there, looking concerned. He put a hand on my shoulder and knelt down so that we were face to face.

"Who has hurt you? I'll kill them with my bare hands," he said with a frown.

I couldn't help but smile the tiniest bit through my tears. "No one has hurt me, Irish, but I appreciate your concern."

"Then what has you so upset?" He sat in the seat beside me and handed me a clean handkerchief. As I dabbed my eyes, I told him about my dream, and about the knowledge that what I'd seen had really taken place, or was about to.

"I know it sounds odd, and I can't explain it very well, but I *know* it's true. I can feel it," I said. My voice cracked a little at the end and I took a deep breath, trying to regain my composure.

"It doesn't sound odd at all," Irish said, and I looked at him curiously. "You're a seer. Of *course* you are! I should have known it when I first saw that rainbow aura of yours."

"What do you mean, a "seer"?" I asked.

"Just as some living people are what they call "clairvoyant", some of us on this side can see things others can't. I've only known one other besides you who had visions, you know. It's quite a rare thing."

"But it wasn't a vision, it was a dream...and besides, I wasn't able to do this when I was alive."

He shrugged good-naturedly, a shrug which said, *I can't explain it, but I know it to be true,* and I saw Ben in the gesture, briefly. Suddenly my heart felt torn in two all over again and a sob rose up in my throat before I could stop it.

"It isn't fair!" I cried. "I've been here all alone for so many years! Where are they? Why was I chosen to come here and not them?"

I covered my eyes for a moment and let my emotions pour out, and after a moment I felt the insubstantial weight of Irish's arm around my shoulders. He murmured soothing words against my ear as I rocked slightly and then leaned into him, needing to feel the comfort of another lost soul.

"I know you miss your family. We are all orphans on this side of things." he said softly, resting his chin upon the top of my head. "But you're not alone, Miss Lucy."

I looked up then and saw the earnestness in his expression and knew I had a good friend in Irish. Suddenly, I felt foolish.

"I'm sorry," I said. "I didn't mean to sound ungrateful. You have been a godsend since I got here...I don't know what would have become of me that first day if I hadn't met you."

He waved a hand dismissively at me and bowed his head in a shy sort of way. I could see I had embarrassed him and wished I could find the words to ease his mind. Instead, I sat back in my seat and looked up at the blank movie screen, sensing a change of subject was in order.

"Sometimes I look up there and I can almost see my life playing across that screen," I said. "I see my family as they were right before I died, and the friends I had, and the memories we made. Sometimes those memories are more painful than they are sweet," I said.

"I know the feeling, Miss Lucy," Irish sighed. "But you can't spend the rest of your days pining for the past. How can you walk forward if you are constantly looking over your shoulder? It's no way to exist."

I pondered this for a moment. "I suppose you're right. It's just...I thought that the pain of losing the people I loved would fade over time. It hasn't faded. Some days, hours will pass without me thinking of my living days, and then all of a sudden the realization that I'm dead will slam back into me and my heart will break all over again."

"I wish I could tell you it gets better."

I turned to him sadly, a question suddenly forming in my mind that hadn't occurred to me until then. "Who did you leave behind, Irish?"

When he spoke, his voice was low and melancholy.

"No one. And sometimes, I wonder which is worse."

****

For weeks after our conversation, I couldn't forget about what Irish had said: that I was a seer. I still wasn't exactly sure what it meant, but it intrigued me and frightened me at the same time. Had I really watched my sister take her last breath in my dreams? If it was true that I held this power, what else would my subconscious mind throw at me?

Not only was I occupied by these worries, I was also becoming more and more obsessed with Archer. Ever since my first glimpse of him, he consumed my thoughts. I couldn't rid myself of the feeling of kinship I felt with him, even though the realistic side of my brain told me over and over that it was impossible; I had fallen hard for an image on a screen, and that's all he was to me.

Still, I couldn't shake that feeling. I hardly left the theater during the run of *Crazy Love,* not wanting to miss any of the showings. When the Imperial finished its run of the picture, I went to every movie house in town until I found one still showing it. I became a woman obsessed, and even though I knew my behavior wasn't normal, I couldn't help myself. I wanted to see as much of Archer as I could. And even after *Crazy Love* left every theater in the city, I was unable to get him out of my mind.

Weeks went by, and then months. Time did not diminish the way I felt for this perfect stranger. I walked around town in a daze with what I'm sure was a dreamy look on my face, and I was so preoccupied with my daydreams that I almost breezed right past Irish one gorgeous Spring morning.

"I've seen that look before," he said. I stopped in my tracks and smiled when I realized I had come close to passing him up.

"Irish," I said. "How have you been?"

"Not as well as you, I'm willing to wager," he said. "You are positively glowing, Miss Lucy, and not just because you have a lovely aura around your head. Found someone you fancy?"

"Why, yes," I said, lowering my head shyly. "Is it that obvious?"

"Only to someone like me, who notices these things. So who is he? Anyone I know?"

I looked around at the people streaming past us on the sidewalk, amazed as I always was at the energy that surrounded the living. It seemed to fly off their skin like sparks in the brilliant morning sunlight.

"You'll laugh," I said.

He swept the black bowler hat off his head and held it over his heart for a moment. "I solemnly swear not to laugh, Miss Lucy."

"Well, I haven't exactly met him yet," I began, watching his face for any sign that he was about to tease me, "But his name is Archer Black. He lives in Los Angeles, California. He's a film star."

"Ah, yes. Archer Black. He's all the rage these days, isn't he?"

"You've heard of him?"

"Hard to avoid him if you spend any time at the theater," Irish said with a little smile. "You said you haven't met him "yet". Does that mean you plan on making a trip to Los Angeles?"

I thought about it for a moment, watching the citizens of New York stream around us on the sidewalk. "I don't know," I said. "I hadn't given it much thought, really. How does someone in our situation take a cross-country trip, anyway?" I couldn't picture myself on an airplane, and a train ride from New York to California would be too long for me to handle.

"Simple, Miss Lucy. You wait for it to rain."

****

The library was so still at midnight that I found myself glad I didn't have to breathe and disrupt the hushed atmosphere. There were a few other ghosts on the third floor and one hovering around the card catalog downstairs--she had been the head librarian for thirty years before she died--but I was all alone on the second floor. I sat at one of the large oak tables and thought about what Irish had told me, about how to travel quickly from one place to another. It sounded intriguing and a bit scary, and I wasn't at all sure yet that it was something I wanted to try, but I couldn't put Archer out of my mind. I still felt that odd kinship with him, so strong it was almost magnetized. Some part of me felt like I was being pushed in his direction, yet I had no idea why it should be so.

I suddenly felt so very tired. Thinking in circles was exhausting, I thought, and laid my head down on the table, wincing as I did. Inanimate objects still felt odd to me, even after so many years of living the life of the undead. The wood was firm but not as hard as it would be to human skin, and yet it still felt insubstantial, as though my head might pop right through it to the other side.

The other side, I thought distantly, still hearing Irish's words jangling in my brain. The other side of the water. The other side of the country.

My mind felt thick with sleep as I began to tumble down that tricky rabbit-hole towards dream country, passing disjointed images as I went: hundreds of lily pads floating on a pond, the surface of the water filled with them. A huge weeping willow tree, it's branches bent to the ground in a graceful arch(Archer), standing alone in the middle of a field.

And a familiar face, one I hadn't seen in so long....Ben. His handsome features were transformed by grief, I saw, and it was my fault. I tried to call out to him, to tell him I was sorry, but he was already gone. And all the while I heard a rushing noise in my ears, a sound like water....the pond? No, the pond was still and silent.

The world turned upside down and for a moment I was strongly disoriented, thrust into a dark place with that roar filling my ears, and then I realized I had done it; I had jumped into a rain- puddle, just like Irish had told me to.

"Now remember, Miss Lucy, don't let your mind tell you something different once you get there," Irish was saying. I recalled him saying these exact words on the sidewalk, yet I could hear them as plainly as if he were right beside me, whispering them into my ear.

"Don't let fear get in the way of what you know to be true. Once you find the right puddle, you must jump in the way you would do in a swimming pool. It will be difficult the first time, because your eyes will tell you it is impossible, that the puddle is simply too shallow. But it is important that you jump and don't just ease yourself in, otherwise you might end up in a sewer somewhere."

"But why?" I had asked with eyes wide. Even after over seventy years of existing as a spirit, I had a lot to learn about the way things worked in our world. *"I mean, couldn't I just think of Los Angeles and appear there?"*

This was the way things were done in our world; I had done it often enough over the years, especially if I was on one side of town and was too tired to walk to the other. It was a convienient mode of transportation; almost like teleportation, I suppose, or what I understand it to be.

Irish had shook his head. *"That's all fine and dandy when you need to take a short trip inside the city limits, but any distance longer than that and things get tricky. No one knows where we go in those few seconds, and I dare to wager no one would ever **want** to know. Who knows what sort of wires could get crossed in that in-between world? You could accidentally* *send yourself to a parallel universe, or alter the course of history. Too tricky, Miss Lucy, much too tricky. I'd stick to puddle-jumping if I were you."*

So I had jumped. I had taken the plunge and now, instead of finding myself in a shallow puddle of rain-water, I was swimming down into the cerulean depths of the Pacific Ocean.

"I wish I could tell you how it works," Irish said on the sidewalk, *"But I can't even guess. It's just one of the many perks we get. You can travel the length of the country in a few short minutes every time it rains here; you just have to know where to look for good, deep puddles. Puddles on the East side of the city take you to the Atlantic Ocean. The ones on the West side take you to the Pacific. Simple enough."*

I had nodded, listening carefully.

"One more thing, Miss Lucy, and this is important, to be sure: you must concentrate on where you want to end up while you swim. Focus your mind as hard as you can, otherwise you'll waste precious time trudging around an unfamiliar city."

I have to concentrate on what I'm doing, I told myself, and fanned my arms out in front of me to propel through the dark water. My ears bore the pressure of all the water above me and I felt real, physical pain for the first time in many years. Slowly, though, the pressure dissipated, and my eyes began to adjust slowly to the dim light. I could see small schools of fish all around me, their colorful little bodies flashing in the light from the surface. I thought of what Irish told me, his careful instructions, but it was impossible to focus on where I wanted to end up. The only thing I saw in my mind's eye was Archer's face.

I had to find him.

****

"Miss Lucy?"

I opened my eyes and was suddenly and dizzyingly disoriented. For a moment I didn't have a clue where I was or how I got there, and then I looked up and saw Irish standing

44

above me. His dark eyes sparkled with good humor, as though it amused him to find me sleeping.

"Hello, Irish," I said, sitting up fully and looking around. The light had changed; night had passed into day as I slept. The library was already starting to swarm with activity.

I suddenly remembered my dream and quickly stood up, taking Irish's arm in my excitement.

"Have you seen a weather report for today?" I asked eagerly.

"Can't say that I have. Does that mean what I think it means?"

I nodded. "I've decided I want to do it, Irish. I want to take a puddle to find Archer Black."

"Well then, I have some good news for you," he said with a smile. "Looks like it doesn't matter if it rains or not. According to the front page of The Post, Archer Black is coming to New York City."

Part Two:
In which we meet some people who will soon change Lucy's world forever

Chapter One
Archer

Archer Black stood at the window in his hotel room, enjoying a panoramic view of London. The rain blurred the edges of things, turning the landscape into a watercolor. He saw that the trees had flipped their leaves up against the wind and was reminded instantly of home, of the way the magnolia trees looked right before a storm. He could almost smell their blossoms, the memory was so real.

He was so homesick someone was going to have to invent a new word for it. It had been two months since he had seen Asheville, North Carolina and the time away from his family was starting to get to him. He had spoken to his mama every night since arriving in Europe, but hearing her voice on the other end of a lot of telephone wires only served to hurt his heart more. The doctors said she had at least another good year or two left in her, but deep down he found he didn't believe that. Even so, she did her best to sound upbeat during their conversations, and he loved her even more for it. If she had given the slightest indication that she wanted him home he would have been on the first plane back to the states, press junkets be damned.

His third (and some critics said his best) movie, *Look West*, had been given a limited screening in Europe a week ago and was receiving rave reviews. He had commanded his highest salary to date, the studio was talking about a sequel to *Crazy Love*, and the name Archer Black had begun to strike women everywhere with gooseflesh. And while all that was more than he had ever hoped for, he was beginning to wonder if it would ever end. He had only been in London for thirteen hours and had already done twenty-five interviews. If he wanted to leave the hotel, a police escort was summoned to keep the paparazzi at bay. It was all just a little overwhelming to a guy who wasn't even old enough to take a legal drink, a guy who was soft-spoken and well mannered because his Mama had raised him that way. He was a true Southern gentleman, but he had to wonder if the life he was living would eventually change him. Some of the things he had seen in Hollywood circles since becoming famous...well, it was behavior he had only read about in magazines. It was all so tiring...the parties, the premieres, the interviews and fashion critiques ("Who are you wearing?" was a question he had never had asked of him until six months ago, and it still amused him that people actually cared about who designed his suits). At the end of the day, all he wanted was a glass of sweet tea and a hammock to lie in.

"That sounds like something out of a Tennessee Williams play," Steven Meyer, his agent, said when Archer expressed his feelings of homesickness over the phone. Steve was in New York, preparing for Archer's return to the states and for the upcoming screening of *Look West* in Manhattan. "Do you people really just lie around in hammocks all the time? I thought that was a stereotype."

"*You people*?" Archer asked. "Your hometown is only two hundred miles from Asheville."

"Yes, but a very important two hundred miles," Steve said.

Archer sighed heavily and sat on the plush leather couch, wishing he could just sprawl out and take a nap. The personal interviews were over with for the day, but he still had a phone-in with a reporter from Japan before he could even grab a bite for dinner.

"I'm just so damned tired," he said, rubbing a hand across his eyes.

"Still not sleeping well?" Steve asked.

"It's the jet-lag. I'll be fine once I get back onto American soil."

He hoped. He had actually parted ways with restful sleep a long time ago, and it had nothing to do with jet lag. It was the dreams; they invaded his subconscious every time he was away from home longer than a couple of days. Sometimes they weren't dreams at all, just maddening snippets of dialogue and images from his childhood, random puzzle pieces scattered across his mind. These things haunted him in waking hours, as well.

Distantly, Archer heard Steve say he hoped that was the case before he moved on to the details of Archer's impending arrival in New York, but Archer's mind was somewhere else, someplace far away, where the smell of honeysuckle assaulted the nose and the lonely sound of a train whistle in the night induced shivers down one's spine. He could see home in his mind's eye; a sprawling log house surrounded by trees and dotted with Kudzu vines on the Western wall. There was a creek that ran through the back of the property and the water always looked silvery, no matter what time of day it was. He could almost smell the metallic scent of it, his mind was so focused on the memory. Past the creek was the barn, which doubled as a garage and almost concealed a path down to the pond. Beyond *that* was an open field, where a lone weeping willow tree held residence. It was enormous, that tree, and spread its branches out over what had seemed like miles when Archer was a boy. To him, that tree was almost the epitome of home; it had given him shade on the hottest summer days, and had wrapped him with cool comfort when he needed it most.

Of course, he couldn't think of home without it bringing an image of his mother to the forefront of his mind, and this, more than anything, made his heart ache. It was familiar, that ache. It spoke of a deep loss, of mourning and grief. It was a feeling he hadn't been able to shed since it's birth when he was just a child, when he first began to see and speak to the ghosts which haunted his family home.

There were two of them, a woman and a man who wore the clothing of a cowboy, and the first time Archer came in contact with the man at the age of ten he had frozen in place on the staircase, too shocked to run for help. It didn't even occur to him to be afraid until much later, when the man had appeared to him again at the foot of his bed and turned suddenly, horrifyingly violent for no apparent reason. He had attacked Archer, leaving awful scratch marks down both of his forearms, and all the boy could do was yank the covers up over his head and try to block the attacks.

49

He had wanted so badly to tell his mother what happened the next morning, but by the time he dressed for school and came to the table for breakfast, it all seemed to float to the back of his mind. By the time he finished his pancakes, he found he could almost believe it was simply something he had seen on television. After all, he couldn't even see the scratch marks, thanks to the long-sleeved shirt he was wearing. In the bright, sunny light of that sweet-smelling April morning, the idea that his house was haunted just seemed silly. And so, following an event that would have sent an adult screaming from the property and into the arms of the nearest psychiatrist, Archer simply went on with his life. It was the sort of defense mechanism employed by children everywhere; ignore it, and it doesn't exist.

By the time he was attacked again some three weeks later he couldn't have told his mother even if he wanted to; she was dealing with the sudden and unexpected death of her husband.

She was a rock through the whole thing. She had buried the love of her life after fifteen years of marriage and never shed a tear at the funeral; the knowledge that she had to be strong for her son was always at the front of her mind, and Archer had sensed that somehow. He felt it in the soft pressure of her hand on his during the minister's prayer, and in the solid comfort of her bosom when he leaned against her after the service. He had been on the verge of breaking down all that afternoon, especially after seeing his father lying motionless in the casket, but the mere touch of his mother gave him an extra boost of strength. They had held each other up on the way out of the church--his arm around her waist, hers across his narrow boy's shoulders--and he had smelled the sweet notes of her favorite perfume, the kind she only wore on special occasions. He knew then that his heart would never be the same. They couldn't go back. So he had clung to his mother the way a drowning man would do a life preserver and breathed in deep, knowing he would never smell that scent on her again; it had been a gift from his father.

And later, long after he went to bed for the night, he lay

awake in the darkness and listened to his mother sob in her room across the hall. He had thought he would never get to sleep, not with all he had seen and everything he had been through over the course of the afternoon, but sheer exhaustion set in after a while and his eyelids drooped closed. The mournful sound of his mother's cries followed him down the path to sleep, and he began to dream immediately. He saw his father as he had been the last time Archer saw him alive: a healthy man in a flannel shirt, rooting through a tool box out in their garage. The two of them had talked that day of the sort of things fathers and sons talk about, school and cars and baseball, and it was this he remembered as he slept; simple, easy conversation. And when Archer awoke at four a.m. to find his father sitting at the foot of his bed, he was not at all surprised. The two of them had continued their conversation as though it was the most normal thing in the world, as though one of them wasn't actually buried beneath six feet of dirt and rocks and grass out at Crestview Cemetary. There was no reason to feel afraid, he knew, because this wasn't like the other times. It was just his father, after all.

****

Later, he was awakened from a light doze to a knock at the door. He stood from the couch and rubbed the back of his hand across his eyes, trying to remember what he'd been dreaming about, but as usual all he got was a vague compilation of images that didn't make much sense when viewed separately. He was beginning to wonder if dreams had the ability to drive a man crazy.

"Mr. Black?"

He peered through the peephole of his hotel room door and saw a bellhop standing in the hallway, holding a brightly wrapped package.

"You didn't have to bring this up, I could have come down to the front desk to get it," Archer said as he pulled the door open. He took the bulky box from the bellhop's arms. It was marked on all four sides with shiny red hearts, the sort you usually find in stores on Valentine's Day. It was obviously a gift from a fan, and Archer groaned inwardly. That meant they had found him, then. There was more than likely a growing line of girls standing outside the hotel, talking to one another in hushed voices, their eyes scanning the windows for any sign of him. *Which one do you think is his room?* he could imagine them whispering. *Is he in there now, having dinner with Jennifer Anniston? Taking a shower?* He knew that with his growing celebrity came a certain measure of privacy loss, but it made him uncomfortable nonetheless.

The young man smiled with an air of sympathy that bespoke several years experience in dealing with overzealous fans--The Four Seasons was well known in London to be a haven for movie stars and musicians--and shook his head.

"Pardon me, sir, but it's much easier to bring things to you than the other way around."

Archer nodded and set the box down to retrieve his wallet, where he kept several bills just for tipping the hotel staff. He had always been a good tipper, and thought it was especially important to continue to do so now that his star was rising in Hollywood; not because he wanted to flaunt his money, but because it was vital to him to show those who didn't know him that he was a nice person, a normal guy from North Carolina who just happened to make movies, not the type of celebrity who expected things to be handed to him by a waitstaff. The last thing he wanted to do was alienate people with his fame. He already felt alien enough.

"Yeah, I guess you're right," he said, handing the bellhop a ten dollar-bill. "Is it a madhouse down there?"

"Oh, not too bad, sir." But Archer could see in the man's face that it *was* bad, and suddenly he felt guilty for making things harder for the hotel staff. The bellhop seemed to sense his subtle change in mood and gave him a reassuring smile.

"If you'd like, I can arrange to sneak you down into the piano bar. There's a kitchen access that only the staff know about--"

"That's not necessary, but thank you. I think I'll just retire for the evening."

The bellhop nodded and thanked him for the tip, which had already been expertly pocketed.

Alone with his gift, Archer stood with his hands on his hips and stared at it. He was always wary of opening gifts from fans, even though his security staff wouldn't allow anything dangerous to get by them. They kept silent vigil downstairs at all times, monitoring everyone and everything that went up to the penthouse. It wasn't just for his safety; the hotel staff greatly appreciated having extra help when a big-name celebrity was staying with them.

It looked innocent enough, he thought, and nudged the box gently with his foot. When nothing happened he picked it up, sat it on the coffee table, and retrieved a knife from the kitchen to split open the tape.

Inside there were layers and layers of red tissue paper. He pulled each one aside until finally, at the very bottom of the box, he came to a small white envelope. "Archer" was written in pink glittery ink on the front. It felt too thick to be just a letter....pictures, maybe? He grimaced and considered putting the envelope back where he'd found it and giving it to his security people to look at. He had a weird feeling about this anonymous gift, a sense of foreboding that made his stomach queasy. But his curiosity was aroused...

He sliced open the envelope and pulled out what was inside: two Polaroid pictures and a small piece of paper.

The first photo was of a girl whose face was obscured by her long, dark hair. She held her hands up to the camera, curling her fingers and thumbs towards each other to make a heart shape. On her right wrist was a tattoo of the initials *A.B.* in curly pink script.

The second photo was of him, sleeping on the couch.

He let out a breath he hadn't realized he'd been holding and dropped the pictures onto the coffee table, wiping his hand absently on his jeans as though he had just touched something slimy. He suddenly felt like he was on an elevator that had dropped three floors with no warning, all weak-kneed and covered in a cold sweat. This was much worse than poisoned treats or even a crazed fan with a gun; someone had violated his space, his privacy, had been in his room while he was asleep...perhaps just mere minutes ago.

But how?

It didn't seem possible, yet he had the proof right here in front of him.

Suddenly he remembered the note and fanned the photos out where they had fallen on the floor until he found the scrap of paper, crumpled up beneath them. He picked it up with hands that were not quite steady.

Don't worry, it said. *I would never hurt you. I'm your biggest fan. P.S.--You are even more adorable when you sleep.* It was signed with a glittery pink heart.

Archer dropped the note and picked up the phone.

****

"I will be cutting my stay here short and catching the redeye to New York tonight," Archer explained to the hotel manager a little later. The manager had been summoned, along with the head of Archer's traveling band of security, Jason Whitestone, to be briefed on what had happened. "It's nothing against you, your staff, or the hotel itself--I've had a great visit --but I can't continue to sleep here knowing that someone got past all the security stationed downstairs. I hope you understand."

The hotel manager, whose shiny gold nametag read V. Cross, nodded emphatically and reached into his pocket for a pen and business card. His face had been purple since Archer had explained what had happened, all the English bluff and hearty banter completely gone. He was mortified, Jason knew, and more than that, he was afraid the press would get hold of the news and ruin the reputation of the hotel he loved more than his own wife. Jason had a knack for sussing people out at a glance this way; it was part of his job, after all. He hoped Mr.

V. Cross didn't have high blood pressure, otherwise he might drop dead before they could get the situation sorted out.

"I completely understand, sir," Cross was saying to Archer, his voice tight with the effort of controlling his emotions. "I want you to know I have my best security men on this. They are looking through all the surveillance tapes as we speak. I hope you won't hold this against us in the future if you should ever need to stay in London."

Archer managed a tight smile and took the business card from him, upon which was scrawled his name and personal phone line should Archer "need anything" the next time he was in town. Jason smirked and folded his arms across his massive chest. *Right*, he thought. *Way to cover your butt.*

"Thanks for your help," Archer, ever the gentleman, said.

"I assure you, we will find out who this person is and she will be banned from this hotel for life. Also, I have already informed the front desk that you are leaving immediately and that you are not to be billed for your stay here."

"Oh, you don't have to do that, really, I--" Archer began

"No, no, I insist, Mr. Black," the manager said, holding his neatly manicured hands up in front of him. "You are a valued customer at The Four Seasons and we want to ensure that you leave with at least that small comfort."

"I appreciate that, Mr. Cross, but I really wouldn't feel right leaving without paying. And I honestly wouldn't have been bothered by the fact that a fan got by security if she had only come to my door. It's the fact that she got in here somehow that makes me uncomfortable. I am a very private person and to have my space invaded...." He trailed off and shook his head, at a loss for words. A man as guarded as he was was afraid of only one thing, and it had happened tonight.

"Of course, Mr. Black. I can assure you, it will never happen again, not while I am head of this hotel."

Archer thanked him again and they exchanged goodbyes. Jason felt sorry for the poor schmucks working for hotel security; someone was going to get reamed tonight.

"We should leave as soon as possible, the flight leaves in

Amanda Crum

two hours and it'll take a while to get the car loaded up and to the airport," Archer said. His bags were already packed and sat beside the door like faithful black dogs.

"You got it," Jason said, already moving toward the door. He stopped short and turned back to Archer with a frown furrowing his brow. "How do you think she got in here? Did you have a window open or something?"

Archer shook his head. "I honestly have no idea. All the windows were closed and locked from the inside."

"Same with the door?"

"Yeah, but the door locks automatically when it closes. Maybe she got a copy of the key card from someone here at the hotel?"

"Maybe. Weird though, isn't it? That she would go to all the trouble to get in here and then just take pictures of you? She won't even have copies of them, because they're Polaroids."

"Strange," Archer agreed. "And more than a little bit creepy."

For Archer, the evening's events had turned into something more than just one fan's desire to meet him; he felt too violated for that to be the case. He'd had that feeling before; not during the poignant late-night talks with his father's spirit, but upon meeting the other ghost residing in his childhood home. The dark one. The one who was so starved for human contact that something in him had turned, making him violent.

****

Outside The Four Seasons, behind the dumpsters in the back, a young woman stood in the shadows. Her long dark hair obscured most of her face, but when she brought a cell phone up to her ear her features were illuminated. She was pretty, with pale skin and blue eyes, and on her wrist was a tattoo.

"Mercy, it went perfectly!" she whispered breathlessly into the phone. "You're a genius!"

"Glad I could be of help, dear," Mercy purred. "Does he know you were in his room?"

56

The girl paused before answering, and Mercy didn't even need to use her psychic abilities to read into that silence.

"What did you do, Darcy?" she asked quietly.

"It was no big deal," Darcy pouted. She pictured Mercy sitting in her favorite purple armchair, stroking her cat and stuffing her face with Twinkies, and smirked. Who was she to judge? Darcy had used the older woman's knowledge to gain access to her favorite star, and now Mercy was condemning her for it? She had no right. "I left him a note, that's all."

"You promised me you wouldn't interfere with his life!" Mercy hissed. "I never would have agreed to giving you that potion if I'd known what you were going to do!"

"Don't be so dramatic!" Darcy said, looking around her to make sure she was still alone. "I couldn't resist. How often does a girl have a chance to sneak into a movie star's hotel room undetected? But don't worry, I got in and out with no problems. The potion worked better than I ever hoped. I was totally invisible for an hour!"

"I hope you know what you're doing, child," Mercy said softly. "These are dangerous waters you're treading in."

"I hate it when you call me child," Darcy said through clenched teeth. "You're not my mother. Besides, it's only fair that I get to introduce myself to him. After all, I *am* his number one fan."

Chapter Two
Mercy and Darcy
Pike's Hollow, Virginia

Mercy Deveroux sat at the kitchen table, looking over the tarot cards fanned out in front of her. She was a large woman, all rounded curves and deep dimples, but somehow this didn't soften her image a bit. She was imposing, with gray frizzy hair and thick black eyebrows set in a perpetual furrow. A large black cat lay purring at her feet, his belly rumbling with the effort. He seemed to complete the picture somehow, Darcy thought; even a modern day witch such as Mercy needed a black cat.

"Well? What do you see?" Darcy asked impatiently, leaning across the table to get Mercy's attention.

"Don't rush me, child," Mercy scolded without looking up. "You're breaking my concentration."

Darcy rolled her eyes and sat back in the kitchen chair, crossing her arms petulantly. "I thought you said you had something to tell me," she said.

Mercy sighed and pushed her graying hair away from her temples, looking up at the girl in irritation. "I do. What you did the other night was totally irresponsible, and if the authorities get hold of you for breaking into Black's room, you're on your own."

Darcy's eyes narrowed in anger. "What do you mean, *the authorities*? Did you hear something?"

"No, there hasn't been a word about it in the media yet, but a star as popular as Archer Black doesn't keep secrets for long. Sooner or later, someone is going to find out that his room was broken into."

"His room wasn't broken into--I stole a keycard from the chambermaid. And I used my laptop to interrupt the signal on the security cameras, just like you told me to. Don't worry, I didn't leave a trace of evidence behind." Not counting the photos she'd sent to him, but she didn't want to tell Mercy about those. It had been impossible to resist at the time, but she knew if the old lady found out about them she would refuse to help with Darcy's next plan, and she needed her for that.

"You listen here, girl," Mercy said, leaning forward. "This is not a joke. I helped you out because your mother was a good friend of mine, and because I wanted to see if that potion really worked. That little vial of liquid is a goldmine, do you understand that? I could sell it to the right people and retire to the Bahamas with the money. I bet the military would pay a pretty penny for a potion that makes the drinker invisible."

"So?" Darcy mumbled. She was barely listening to Mercy anymore; her mind had moved on to a memory that had sprung up at the mention of her mother, who had committed suicide when Darcy was nine years old.

She had come home from school on that horrific day to find a plate of chocolate chip cookies on the table, which was odd; her mother usually didn't allow Darcy to have excessive sweets. There was no note, and the house seemed empty; her father wasn't home yet, which was also odd. He set his own hours as a real estate agent and was almost always home to greet her when she got off the bus. Thinking her mother must be in the bath, Darcy skipped upstairs (after slipping a cookie off the plate), threw her backpack unceremoniously on her bed, and went into her parent's bedroom. It was empty, with the bed neatly made and the windows thrown open. A light breeze, redolent of the sweet scent of newly mown grass, fluttered the curtains and lifted Darcy's hair off her forehead.

"Mom?" she called. "You in here?"

The door to the attached bathroom was open slightly. She pushed it forward and saw her mother in the bathtub, leaning back against the blue tile wall with her eyes closed.

"Mom, you shouldn't fall asleep in the tub, it's dangerous," Darcy began, but as she walked closer she saw the bottle of pills clutched in her mother's hand and knew she wasn't just asleep. Her chest wasn't moving up and down with the rhythm of her breathing and her eyelids looked funny; they were shiny and pale blue, almost the exact same color as the tile on the wall behind her.

"Mom?" she had whispered shakily. "Mommy?"

"Are you listening to me?" Mercy said, cutting into Darcy's memory. "Or am I wasting my breath?"

Darcy sighed heavily and pushed away the image of her mother's face. "I'm listening."

"I didn't invite you over just to scold you. I have another experiment for us to try."

Mercy lifted the lid on a large wooden box that sat on the table and brought out a small bottle of cloudy pink liquid, very similar to the one Darcy had ingested in order to become invisible. Next to this she placed a much smaller vial, about the size of a perfume sample, filled with something blue that gave off a faint glow.

"What's with the blue stuff? It looks radioactive," Darcy said, reaching out to touch the glass vial. Mercy slapped her hand away.

"You aren't to touch it, do you hear me? It is a thousand times more dangerous than the other potion."

"Alright, alright, you don't have to get violent," Darcy said through her teeth.

"I will handle it until the time comes for you to use it. Until then, don't even look at it too closely."

"Well? Don't keep me in suspense! What is this fabulous experiment?"

Mercy smiled and indicated the tarot cards she had laid out before her. "I did a reading for you to make sure the conditions are right to move on with what I have in mind, and it looks like it will work out perfectly. Of course, it will require your dedication and *discretion*, child. Those things are most important."

"For heaven's sake, Mercy, just spit it out already," Darcy said, exasperated.

Mercy pursed her lips, clearly irritated at being interrupted, but went on anyway. "The blue liquid is something I have been working on for years. I've never been able to get the formula right, but last week I had a breakthrough in my calculations and

I think I cracked it. However, I need to test it out. That's where you come in. I need you to use the invisibility potion to get inside the funeral home and place some of this liquid on the tongue of a corpse."

Darcy sat back in her seat, stunned. "You want me to do *what*?"

"It sounds worse than it is," Mercy said, waving a hand dismissively at Darcy. "It will only take a few minutes and I'm prepared to pay you."

"Why would you want to mess with the dead? That's so creepy," Darcy said with a shudder.

Mercy's eyes narrowed. "I am a medium. I take my job very seriously, and when the dead speak to me they almost always need my help. I have to try my best to help them, because I am all they have. It's not everyone who can communicate with the other side." What she didn't mention was that she had already tried the blue potion on someone...and the results were perplexing, to say the least.

Darcy sat back in her chair, wondering if Mercy had ever spoken to her mother. She had never really given it much thought before now. For a moment she was speechless, a rarity for her, and she considered asking the old lady if she had been in contact with her mom. But then she decided she didn't want to know.

"So....why can't you just do it yourself?" she asked finally.

"I can't drink that pink stuff. It takes a lot out of a person to become invisible, and it takes a toll on you physically. My heart is too weak to mess with it. I'm not a young woman anymore," she added sadly.

Darcy thought about it for a moment. She couldn't imagine touching a dead body; on the other hand, Mercy had mentioned something about paying her, and that was something she couldn't ignore.

"If I agree to do this, I want your word that you'll stay out of my business," she said finally. "That means no more lectures, and I especially don't want to hear any more of your opinions on Archer."

Mercy inclined her head, her lips still pursed. "Fine. What about the payment? We should get that out of the way."

Darcy shook her head. "I don't want your money. What I want in exchange for doing this is a small supply of the invisibility potion."

Mercy breathed in sharply and narrowed her eyes, ready to say no immediately, but then remembered what she was asking of Darcy. It was enough that she wasn't going to the police; it was probably worth it to make up a batch of the elixir in lieu of a monetary payment. If that was all it took to have her experiment carried out, then so be it.

"Fine," she said. "I'll have it ready in the morning. I'll need you to go to the morgue tonight."

"And," Darcy continued, "I have something I need your help with. You might call it a little insurance policy."

"Something to do with Archer, I suppose?"

"Maybe," Darcy said with a little smile. And, perhaps too late, something occurred to her.

"What exactly does this blue potion do, anyway?"

Mercy smiled, her lips stretching out over her teeth in a slow grin that made Darcy uncomfortable.

"Why Darcy, you're a smart girl. I would have thought you'd figured that out by now." She picked up the tiny vial of liquid and held it up, so that the light from the overhead lamp illuminated it. It was filled with a cold blue light that seemed wrong somehow. Darcy couldn't pinpoint what it was but she knew she would never touch that bottle with her bare hands.

"It awakens the dead," Mercy finished.

*****

Later, after Darcy had gone home for the night, Mercy sat in her favorite rocking chair beside the front window and watched inky clouds gather together as though pulled by an invisible magnet. She rocked slowly, her mind unfocused on anything in particular. Sometimes she did this at bedtime, allowing her thoughts to spread out and away from her to land wherever they fell. Sometimes she was able to see things which hadn't happened yet but surely would; she had been blessed with the ability since she was very young, and tarot cards weren't always necessary. Sometimes she seemed to hear a group of people who could not be seen, perhaps spirits with nowhere to land who wanted to be heard. It should have been frightening, but was not. To Mercy's detached mind, floating as she was in that odd land between awake and asleep, it was just something that happened sometimes.

But sometimes, sitting in quiet repose and allowing herself to drift led her to recall memories she didn't allow herself to think of often. She thought of her family, of things that had happened when she was young, before her body had become old and began to betray her the way bodies sometimes do.

And sometimes, those memories led to good ideas.

*****

Mercy Lillian Daniels was born on the thirty-first of August, 1958, in the midst of the most wrathful thunderstorm to hit the town of Memphis in ten years. It struck around noon, a real wailer, complete with hail and lightning and thunder with enough bass to shake the pictures off the walls of the trailer she was born in; her grandma's house.

Her mama, Augusta, would pretend to be exasperated when Mercy requested to hear the story of her birth, since she asked for it every night before bed until she was ten.

"Again?" she would ask, clicking her tongue. "Aren't you tired of hearing about yourself yet?"

But even she had to admit that it had been impressive and terrifying, having a child rip its way from her womb while the earth soaked up what the heavens poured down in copious amounts. There was something about the magic of thunderstorms that had aways fascinated Mercy; the way the winds could rip up a tree that had been standing for hundreds of

63

years, or the way the rain could swell a river so quickly that people got stuck in the flood just coming home from the grocery store. She used to imagine that she had been spawned from fierce tornadoes, that at the moment of her birth a funnel cloud had formed and touched down in honor of her.

Her mama smiled at the idea; that her daughter had been created by the wind and rain was laughable, to say the very least. But sometimes, she'd say to Mercy's daddy, sometimes she would see the child at play or concentrating on something and then, well, she could almost believe it. Mercy had been blessed with long, unruly hair the color of the heavens at midnight, her eyes the turbulent shade of violet blue that marks the sky for a thunderstorm. It was easy for her mama to picture a blackbird taking flight against violent-colored clouds when she looked at Mercy, easy to imagine her baby being borne from wind and sky. She herself had hair of a shade commonly called "dishwater blonde" and her husband bore the dark red hair of his Irish predecessors, so Mercy's coloring was an anomaly.

Mable, Mercy's grandmother, had been convinced from the very day of her birth that she was special, and not just because of her looks. She had been born with the umbilical cord wrapped around her neck four times and still come out fighting; she had "Looked that bastard Death in the eye and told him to back off", as Grandma Mable was fond of saying when she told the story to anyone who would listen. Mercy always took a certain kind of pride in this, mostly because Grandma Mable became one of her favorite people very early in life, and to be on the receiving end of high praise from her was the same as shaking hands with the president. Of course, her brand of praise usually contained no fewer than two expletives.

Mercy's mama was horrified by her mother's foul mouth but Mercy loved it. Her daddy's mother was a lovely woman in her own right but had very specific ideas of how a lady should behave, and Mercy always felt like she was walking on eggshells when she visited her house.

"Don't say "ain't"," her mama would warn before a visit to

Nana Daniels'. "She hates that. Say "please" and "thank you". And I don't want to hear about you using her good sheets to build a fort, young lady, do you hear me?"

She was terrified of her mother in law, for reasons Mercy wouldn't understand until she was much older. As a child she just assumed that her Nana intimidated everyone in equal amounts.

Grandma Mable, however, was a different story. She cursed like a sailor and smoked an intricately carved wooden pipe filled with a sweet smelling tobacco; she adopted stray cats at an alarming rate and named them after silent film stars; she read tarot cards and tea leaves; she almost always wore head-to-toe purple; and when Mercy was allowed to sleepover at her house she could stay up as late as she wanted and eat whatever her heart desired. If she wanted brownies and lemonade for lunch, that's what Grandma made. If she wanted chips and dip for supper, that's what she got. Grandma was nothing like her own mother; she was the exact opposite of Nana Daniels. There was a certain freedom about her, the feeling that if she got the notion to hop in her car on a Tuesday afternoon and drive two states over for some barbecue, she could-and by-God-would.

Such was not the case with anyone else in Mercy's family. Perhaps because of the lack of any sort of structure in her own childhood, her mama made it her mission in life to plan out every second of every day. Mercy grew up having everything scheduled for her; activities, meals, classes, even play time. Sometimes she longed to be on the road with her dad, who was a musician in a country band. In his life, nothing was planned. There were nights when the wind blew cruelly against her bedroom window, whistling a haunting tune that she could imagine coming from her dad's old Gibson guitar, and she would lie awake and picture him onstage. She could see herself sitting just beyond the curtain, out of the audience's sight-line but with a clear view of the band. She could smell the mingled scents of perfume and spilt beer, could see the way the stage lights cast shadows on her daddy's face and made him look older. She would fall asleep with his voice in her ears and wake up with a damp pillow.

Grandma Mable knew how to make her forget how much she missed him, though.

"Let's build a fort," she'd say, completely out of the blue, and so they would. Sheets and a few chairs were all it took, and then they could lie on their bellies and listen to the rain spatter across the tin roof of her trailer. They could doze or eat chocolate chip cookies or talk about music, which was always a topic Mercy was eager to discuss.

There were days which would pass by almost unnoticed by Mercy when her father was on the road, days she spent sitting at the window in her bedroom getting lost in a book. The summer days never meant much to her as a child; they were only a brief respite from the monotony of school. She skipped two grades in elementary school on the advice of her teachers; they understood that she was far too advanced for their classes, that they couldn't give her what she needed. She was too smart for her own good, her mama always said, but it was hardly Mercy's fault that class bored her almost to tears. Her daddy saw to it that she learned to read at the age of three and she took to it like a duck to water, devouring anything and everything in the house with the written word on it. From there it was simply a matter of her mind progressing, soaking up information like a sponge. He wanted her to be more advanced than he had been at her age; he wanted to challenge her so that she would never accept simply being average. In a way, he saw his daughter as a tiny mold of him, only she would go to college as he hadn't, she would ensure her future as something stable instead of a paycheck-to-paycheck existence. He had grown up impoverished with a single mom and a ghost of a father, he had been given nothing easily in life and had managed to forage something meaningful from it anyway. While he wasn't always able to provide the very best or the most expensive, Mercy sure didn't want for anything as a child.

He was gone a lot, on the road with his band, but Mercy never held it against him. He was doing what he loved, making a living by spinning songs from his fingers, weaving a tapestry of emotion with the strings of his instruments. He would be on the road until October 1st and then the band would take a rest for a few weeks before going back at it. Those days were the best in her young mind; the afternoons were cooler and the sun always seemed to be ready to set even in the early afternoon, casting its reddish glow upon everything beneath it. The nights were always tinged with the scent of burning leaves and the sky seemed heavy with stars. She would sit in her dad's lap before bedtime, watching a bit of television or listening to The Woodsongs Old Time Radio Hour. There were laughter-filled supper times and Saturday morning pancake breakfasts. They had the good clean scent of a man around the house again, the smell of his shaving cream and the lemony cologne he wore. Her mama was happy, for a change.

But eventually he would have to leave again, and things went back to the way they were: silent meals at a dinner table that seemed far too big without him, a house filled with the belongings of women and with their scents, perfume and deodorant and nail polish. Even doing the laundry was depressing, because all the clothes were either Mercy's or her mama's. None of her daddy's flannel shirts or long underwear. Some nights it seemed he would never come home again, that he had only been a big bearded figment of her imagination.

On Thanksgiving the year Mercy turned thirteen, her mama announced she was pregnant.

And then, a year later, a truck driver fell asleep at the wheel in the mountains of West Virginia and Mercy's life changed forever.

*****

There were many things she loved about her Grandma Mable's house; one of her favorites, however, was the huge old weeping willow tree which stood in her backyard. It had been many things for her over the years of her childhood: a clubhouse, a respite from the heat, a friend which embraced her with cool sympathy after her father died. She retreated there often in the days following his funeral, sitting beneath the green boughs and watching dappled sunlight dance across the grass. No one ever bothered her there, and she felt safe in laying back in the cool grass to grieve and doze as she saw fit. It seemed, in those early days of mourning, that she could never get enough sleep.

One afternoon, after she had cried herself into a fitful sleep beneath the tree's shimmering leaves, she awoke to a shadow falling over her face. At first, before she opened her eyes, she assumed a cloud had passed over the sun. She felt a shiver work its way through her even though the day was hot and humid and opened her eyes slowly, trying to fight the feeling that it was more than a cloud and not succeeding.

It wasn't a cloud. It was a man. Rather, he had once been a man.

She lay where she was, bringing a hand up to her face to shade her eyes, trying to focus on his face, but his features were little more than a shadowy blur against the bright backdrop of the summer day.

"Why're you cryin'?" he asked in a deeply Southern accent. "You're far too pretty to be so upset."

Something about his voice made Mercy want to scream. It sounded much too deep to be coming from human vocal chords, and was almost...bubbly, as though he was talking through a mouthful of blood.

"Who are you?" she found herself asking, and almost clapped her hand over her mouth in fear. She hadn't known she was going to speak until the words were already out.

"Just a friend," the man who wasn't a man said.

"Mercy? Where are you, girl? It's almost time to eat!" Grandma Mable had called then, and though Mercy turned her head for just a moment in the direction of her voice, when she looked back the man was gone.

She sat still for a moment, in a state of shock, and it came to her that she had just been visited by someone who had perhaps been there all along. Sometimes, she knew from her

Grandma Mable, the death of someone close to you brought souls from all over who wanted something from the living. The grieving process opened one up, in a way.

And on the heels of that thought came another, more disturbing one: where was her father? If lost souls were going to make a beeline to her because she'd just lost someone, *where was the man who'd started it all?*

It would be a good many years before she came up with an answer, and many more after that before she found a solution. In the meantime, her heart was changed. She found that the more she conversed with the dead--and it happened often, as she had known it would after her father died--the more a little piece of her died inside. It was a necessary evil, she thought, to protect oneself against the pain and horror that came with being blessed with second sight.

But the more she lost those little pieces of herself, the harder it was to go back, until finally--when she was well into adulthood--she realized that if she could see into her own soul she would find a black and tangled mess, deadened like the roots of a diseased tree.

She would never be the same.

Chapter Three
Archer

From 20,000 feet in the air, New York looked impossibly tiny.

Millions of lights twinkled on the ground, mimicking those in the atmosphere around the plane Archer was in. They had begun their descent and would land at La Guardia shortly. The knowledge made him antsy. Airports, especially ones in big cities, were not his favorite places. Papparazzi always swarmed around, following him down the corridors, which only attracted attention from fans. Right now he wished he had thought to pack a disguise.

Instead, he pulled his Knicks cap down over his eyes and tried not to look too conspicuous as he stepped off the plane. He'd instructed Jason to keep a safe distance from him as they walked through the airport to the baggage claim; he attracted almost as much attention as Archer did, with his bulging muscles and dark sunglasses.

Shockingly, no one approached him as he made his way through the security checkpoints, although he did notice several people glance at him and do a double take, as if they were trying to discern whether he was who they thought he was. The security guards checked his I.D. and waved him through discreetly, and for that he was profoundly grateful. All he wanted was to get to his apartment and crash for several hours in total anonymity. Just thinking about it made him walk faster, until he was finally at the baggage claim. And just when he was about to congratulate himself on making it all the way through an airport without being noticed, he heard a shriek.

"Archer Black!"

He turned around and saw two teenage girls standing behind him, nearly vomiting in excitement.

"Hi," he said, giving them a smile. "Listen, I'm kind of in a hurry, so--"

"Could we just get a picture?" the girl on the left said. She

70

was wearing a Twilight t-shirt and had an unfortunate amount of braces on her teeth.

"And an autograph, I can't let you leave without getting an autograph," her blonde friend said flirtatiously.

"Okay," he said with a little laugh. He posed for the camera, first with the blonde while her friend snapped a picture, and then they traded places.

"We are such big fans," the blonde gushed, handing him a scrap of paper and a pen from her purse. "You just don't even know how many times we've seen *Crazy Love!*"

"Well, I appreciate that," Archer said, looking around to see how many people were watching. Several travelers were standing in a little huddle beside the baggage carousel, talking in hushed voices and smiling in his direction. He finished signing his name for the girl with the braces just as several flashbulbs went off in his peripheral vision; the photogs had found him.

"Here you go," he said, handing over his autograph. "Thanks for watching!"

"We love you!" the blonde said as he yanked his bags off the carousel and made his escape. More people had recognized him, he realized, and were stopping to look as several members of the paparazzi ran after him, snapping away with their cameras. He made it to the ticket counters and jumped over the turnstyle, glad to be away from the crowd. He always felt naked when people watched him so closely, naked and vulnerable and unbelievably dorky.

He stopped in the lobby for a moment and checked his voicemail while Jason went outside to hail a cab; there was one message from his agent, assuring him that damage control was already underway in London and that the story of what had happened was (so far) being successfully kept from the media. Archer was to call him the next morning to go over his new itinerary.

Relieved that things were going so smoothly, he pocketed his phone and made his way outside through the revolving door.

Amanda Crum

He was blissfully unaware that a young dead girl followed him right to the awaiting taxi cab.

****

Later, he dreamt of his childhood home.

He saw the weeping willow tree once more, standing silent sentry in an early morning fog. The sky still held stars from the previous night, winking at him through thick clouds that seemed pregnant with rain. He walked towards the pond, which was full of lily pads on the outer banks, and felt his stomach tighten into a slick knot. He felt sure that someone would be waiting for him at the shore.

But no one was there. The grass surrounding the water was untrampled by human feet as well, reassuring him that no one had been here recently. He knelt down on one knee and picked up a flat rock, skimmed it across the placid surface of the pond. It bounced several times before dropping into the depths with a *plonk!* sound. He watched it fall for a couple of feet before it disappeared. For some reason it made him think of a body falling into water, landing with a splash and then being dragged down unceremoniously into the murky fathoms, never to be seen or heard from again.

He began to feel as though someone was watching him. It was an uncomfortable feeling that made the tiny hairs on the back of his neck stand up. He turned slowly to scan the land behind him, certain he wouldn't find anyone; he was spooked by his own melancholy thoughts, that was all.

The dead man sat on a large rock, just to the left of the willow tree.

Archer jumped up, his heart a dull throb in his throat. It was the man who had haunted him as a child, the one who had attacked him. He was hunched over, feet planted firmly on the ground with his elbows resting on his knees. His pale hands hung down like dead birds. Dark, greasy hair hung in lank strips over his black eyes. He stared at the ground between his feet.

72

"Hello," the man said without looking up.

Archer didn't speak. He hadn't seen this man since he was a child, yet he felt the old horror flooding back, reaching into the cockles of his heart and pushing a hot, metallic bile up into his throat.

"Been waitin' for you," the dead man said. He raised his head slowly to look Archer in the eye.

"I don't live here anymore," Archer said softly. And, although there wasn't much that scared him as a grown man, the old fear had returned swiftly and settled in his stomach. "You can't do anything to me."

"Maybe. Maybe not. We can sure find out, though, can't we?" He chuckled, a sound like water gurgling down a dirty drain.

"Why are you bothering me? I didn't do anything to you. I don't even know why you're here," Archer said, suddenly angry. "It's not my fault you're stuck with the living."

"No one knows why they're anywhere, boy. Dead, living, it's all the same."

He stood up then, tossing his hair back so that Archer could see the cold glint of his dead eyes, and walked closer. His boots squished and squelched in the mud.

"I *bother* you because I got nothin' better to do," he said. He was close enough now for Archer to smell his breath. It reeked like a rotting thing, hanging in the air like an infected cloud. "Because you can see me and hear me. I can yell all I want at the living, curse them up one side and down the other, and they don't know the difference. But you--" He reached out and tapped Archer on the chest. "You can hear what I got to say. You can see the anger on my face. You felt the bruises I put on your body when you was just a child. Ain't nobody done any of them things in a lot of years, boy. And it feels good."

"I'm not your whipping boy," Archer snarled, smacking the dead man's hand away from him. He expected backlash and was prepared to block any blows, but to his great surprise, the dead man began to laugh. It was a horrible sound, much like the noise a swarm of bees makes when they are angry. It made

Archer want to cover his ears.

"Oh, that is sweet," the man said, slapping his thigh as he laughed. He staggered back to his rock and collapsed onto it, bellowing out great guffaws as he did so. Archer had no choice but to stand where he was, confused and angry, wishing the man would come back and fight; his fists itched to land a punch on his pallid, pock-marked face. Finally, after a few moments, the man began to wind down. He wiped his eyes and regarded Archer with a faint grin.

"Oh, that sure was sweet," he repeated. "I have to thank you for that one, boy. I haven't had reason to laugh like that in a long time."

"You're not messing with a child anymore," Archer said through his teeth. "I'm not afraid of you. And I don't mind if you find that funny. Your sense of humor will only leave you unguarded and unprepared when I beat the shit out of you."

"Oh, don't get your drawers in a bunch. I was just laughing at your little "whipping boy" comment because this ain't the first time I've heard that."

"I'm sure," Archer murmered with a frown.

"Although I have to say," the dead man continued, "I think I liked it better when it came from your daddy."

****

Archer thrashed his way into consciousness and sat up in a damp puddle of sheets. The dream still had hold of him and for a moment he wasn't sure where he was; then he looked around and recognized the bulky shapes of his bedroom furniture, emerging from the shadows in the pale pre-dawn light coming in through the window.

"My God," he murmured, pressing his hand to his eyes. What a nightmare that had been! And it had been so real, the entire thing...as though he had been magically transported to his childhood home. It was unlike any dream he had ever had, that was for sure.

Still exhausted but knowing sleep wouldn't come easily

again for some time, Archer swung his legs over the bed and stood up with difficulty. His entire body hurt, as though he were 70 instead of 20. This was the price of nonstop travel and work, he thought. If he felt this tired already, what would he feel like when he really was 70?

He didn't know, but he did know that a hot shower was in order if he wanted to feel human again. He made his way into the bathroom, never noticing the dead girl who sat patiently in the corner, watching him with reverence in her eyes. She decided to leave while he was in the shower; as much as she wanted to stay with him, she felt it was wrong to be around while he was doing such a personal thing as bathing.

When he emerged in a cloud of steam, the room was a little brighter; the sun had made its way up over the horizon, breaking through the clouds to stream into his apartment. He sat on the edge of the rumpled bed and dialed his agent, Steven Meyer.

"Good morning," Steven answered, sounding much more awake than was appropriate considering the early hour.

"What are you doing up this early on a Saturday? I was just going to leave you a voicemail," Archer said.

"The wife has me going to a sunrise spinning class with her," Steven said. "We just finished up. It's awesome exercise, great for the calf and thigh muscles."

From the tone of his voice, Archer could tell his wife was within earshot. He grinned and padded into the kitchen to forage for food.

"How much coffee did it take to make you sound like this? You're all energetic, it's totally unlike you."

"I haven't had any coffee yet. Drank six Red Bulls during the class, though."

"Nice. So, any word on my uninvited guest?"

"Hang on, let me go into my office."

That was the great thing about his manager, Archer thought; he was completely discreet about everything. He never had to worry about his reputation with Steve in charge of his career, unlike some members of young Hollywood, whose agents were quick to choose money over loyalty.

After a moment, Archer heard a door close in the background and the squeak of Steve's desk chair as he sat down.

"I spoke to Riley Adkins, the head of security at The Four Seasons," Steve said, getting right to business. Archer, whose stomach was making hideous noises, found a lone Hot Pocket hiding in the back of the icebox and investigated for freezer burn. Seemed okay. "He said they went over every surveillance tape from every camera in the hotel during your entire stay there, but they never saw anyone enter your room except you and the chambermaid, a Miss Dolores Crenshaw. She was interviewed last night and released; she's been on staff for fifteen years and never had even one infraction. Besides, she wasn't anywhere near your room during the time you say you were asleep, and she has witnesses to that affect."

"How is it possible that someone got in without showing up on *one* of the surveillance tapes? There was only a window of about thirty minutes that she could have come in, taken a picture of me while I was asleep, and left. Plus, she would have had to put the package together." He thought for a moment. "Did they check the tapes from the front desk? Maybe whoever left the box is on them."

"Riley said that the box was found sitting in the lobby amongst several other packages and luggage from guests who were checking in. Your name was written on the outside of it, so they let our security guys scan it with the metal detector and then brought it up to you. There was a rush of activity around that time, with people checking in at the desk and bellhops moving baggage around, so there isn't a clear view of any one person on the tapes who could have sat that particular package down."

Archer was silent for a moment, pondering. It was all so strange, so creepy. As though a ghost had visited him. Suddenly, the thought of eating made him want to vomit. He plucked the Hot Pocket from the microwave and tossed it in the trash.

"One weird thing they did find, though," Steve went on, "Is that there was an apparent power surge or something around the time you were asleep. From eight twenty to eight twenty-two p.m., every surveillance camera on your floor lost their signals. All that shows up on the tapes is a blackout."

"Only the ones on my floor, huh? Do you think it's possible that someone messed with the cameras during those two minutes in order to get into my room undetected?"

"I've been thinking about that," Steve said, and Archer could hear the distinct sound of him lighting up a cigar. Great way to balance out that spinning class, Archer thought. "I guess it's possible, but why go to all that trouble and only black out the cameras on one floor? Surely she--I'm assuming it was a girl--would know *all* the tapes would be looked at later, not just those on that particular floor, so anyone going near you would be a suspect. Besides, it would have taken whoever it was more than two minutes to get from the lobby up to your room, take the pictures, and then sneak back out without anyone noticing, and the elevator operator said he didn't take anyone up to your floor that night but the chambermaid--Miss Crenshaw--and the bellhop who brought you the package. Miss Crenshaw went up during her appointed rounds at six o'clock and brought you towels, correct?"

"Yes, that sounds about right."

"So she was the only person on the penthouse level other than the bellhop, who came after the fact anyway."

Archer sighed and scrubbed a hand over his face. His head hurt. "None of this makes sense."

"I know. But listen, don't lose any sleep over this. I'll do whatever I have to do to ensure nothing like this ever happens again. If it means beefing up security, then that's what we'll do."

"Ah, come on, Steve, I already don't like traveling with the entourage I have now--"

"I know it makes you uncomfortable, Archer, and I respect that. But let me tell you this: you are an *international star* now. That comes with a certain amount of...not danger, exactly, but,

I don't know...responsibility. There are going to be a few crazies out there. There's no way around that, and we can't pick them out of a crowd, unfortunately. So you do what you have to do to keep yourself and the people around you safe. There's no turning back, Archer. I don't want to freak you out, but...that's the way it is."

"I guess I know that. I don't want to be a pain, and I really don't want to seem ungrateful....I am so lucky to have this life. It's just taking me a little while to get used to everything, that's all."

"No worries," Steve said. "You're not the first celebrity to have those feelings, trust me. Listen, I've gotta run, I can hear the wife calling me. God only knows what sort of elaborate torture she has planned for me for the rest of the weekend."

Archer smiled. "Good luck with that."

"Thanks. If you need anything don't hesitate to call. I'll fax over your itinerary right now. Not much has changed. We've just had to move up the dates of a couple of things, and your appearance on The Tonight Show has been moved back a week. They've had to rearrange their guest lineup because of a scandal, or something."

"Sounds good."

"Get some rest, the next few weeks are gonna be hectic. Oh, and don't look out your window."

"I will...wait, what?"

But Steve was already gone. Archer hung up, walked slowly over to his window and pulled back the curtains to find two black cars with heavily tinted windows sitting down on the street below. He couldn't see who was inside but was willing to bet it was the new "beefed up security" Steve had mentioned. Shaking his head, Archer found a bottle of aspirin and dry swallowed two of them before laying back down. His head was pounding.

****

Lucy sat in the plush leather chair in the corner of Archer's bedroom, watching him sleep for the second time that day. He seemed not to feel well; she had been there when he'd taken aspirin before falling onto the bed and covering his eyes with his forearm. She had watched him from the shadows in the hallway, afraid to get too close to him. He was unlike other living people, and not just because he was famous. She felt drawn to him, compelled to know him, and that feeling was stronger than anything she had ever felt. It frightened her.

As soon as she was sure he was asleep, she moved silently to the chair in the corner across from his bed and watched him for a moment. His eyelids moved rapidly back and forth as he dreamed, and Lucy thought she would give anything to know what he was dreaming about....

****

Archer found himself back at the pond and cursed under his breath. He'd hoped he had seen the last of this place in his dreams for a while, but it seemed the dead man had more to say to him.

However, when he turned away from the water he found someone else standing beside the tree: the woman who had haunted his childhood home along with the angry cowboy. Christina.

"What are you doing here?" Archer asked. He wasn't sure if he was pleased to see her or not. Whenever the two of them had talked when he was a boy, his stomach had been clenched into a slick knot the entire time, waiting for the man to show up and ruin things. Yet he never did, and Archer hadn't wondered why that was before this moment.

"I overheard what happened earlier," Christina said. She looked exactly the same as he remembered her; same long dark hair, fair skin, dark doe eyes. But then, why would she have changed?

"You mean between me and..." He trailed off, realizing he had never known the dead man's name.

"Dean," Christina supplied.

"His name is *Dean*?"

She smiled slightly. "Did you have another name in mind?"

"Oh, I don't know. Satan, perhaps? Or maybe Marlboro or Dalton or something. He sure doesn't look like a Dean. Maybe if he had a v-neck sweater and a pair of chinos on, I could accept it."

"I don't understand the reference."

Of course she wouldn't, Archer thought. She'd been dead for over a hundred years, if he was judging correctly by her clothing. Chinos hadn't even been invented when she was living.

"Never mind," he said, moving closer to her. He gestured to the large rock where, not long ago, Dean had sat and laughed at Archer's words. "Have a seat."

She lowered herself gracefully onto the rock and clasped her hands in front of her. "I'm sorry for eavesdropping. It was unintentional, I promise. Dean and I have been here together so long that I don't even think twice about keeping track of where he is anymore, I just follow him. When I see that he is occupied with something, then I know it's safe."

"Safe to do what?"

She turned to him, tilting her chin to look into his eyes as he stood beside her.

"Exist," she said softly.

Archer let that sink in. "When I was younger, I never asked why you two were stuck here. I'm not sure why."

"For the same reason you never asked his name," Christina said. "Because knowing would have made it all the more real. No one wants to admit they are being haunted, least of all a child."

There was a certain amount of truth to that. "I guess you thought I was rude."

"Not at all, Archer. I thought you were a very sweet boy."

"Well, I'm glad. I liked your visits a lot."

She smiled and there was a moment of comfortable silence before he went on.

"I know it's a little late, and if my question is too personal,

80

you don't have to answer. But I would like to know about your life. And Dean's, I suppose."

"Better late than never," Christina said. "And it's not too personal. Our story is a simple one. Sad, but simple." She seemed to gather her thoughts for a moment before going on. "I met Dean when I was just a girl, fifteen or sixteen. His family lived down the road from mine, and we went to the same school. He seemed set on me right from the start, and that was fine with me. He came from a good family and my parents approved of him. He treated me with kindness and told me he would take care of me, and I believed him. We married on the day after my eighteenth birthday."

"Wow," Archer whispered. "So young."

"Yes. Too young, really, but in those days that was how it was done. His father gave us a little bit of money he had saved up, and we bought our first home. It stood right over there."

She gestured toward the barn.

"I didn't know anything was built on this land other than our house," Archer said in surprise.

"It was lovely, made of gray stone. We had a great fireplace in the kitchen with a beautiful hearth. I made all of our meals there."

She paused and looked out over the water, and Archer could see great sadness fill her dark eyes. He could almost feel it, himself.

"We were happy, for a time. But in the summer of 1906, Dean lost his job at the paper mill. The company closed down, laying off more than 200 people, and there weren't many jobs going around. He found work at the stockyards, but he hated it. Every night he would come home and drink until he fell asleep. I knew things were bad, but I suppose I thought we would get through it, that he would eventually find work in another town and if we had to move, so be it. That's why, when I found out I was pregnant that winter, I told him right away. I thought the news would cheer him up."

Archer felt a lump rise in his throat. He knew what was coming.

"I was wrong," Christina said. "He was furious when he found out. He said there was no way we could afford a child, not on his salary. We argued. He hit me for the first time that night."

A single tear slid down her cheek.

"The more he drank, the angrier he became. He was out of control. I couldn't fend him off, not when he was in that condition. He beat me so badly that I...I lost the baby."

"I'm so sorry, Christina," Archer said softly, but she gave no notice that she heard him. She continued to look out over the water, a distant expression on her face. She was there, reliving those events, even though her spirit sat beside him. In her mind, it must have felt like that day had just recently passed.

"I hated him after that. How could I forgive him?" She paused then and looked at Archer, her eyes full of anger and disgust and sadness and longing. Something about the way she said that last sentence made it seem like a plea, as though she was asking for validation that whatever she felt was right. He had the sudden urge to hold her but kept his distance.

"He took something from me that he had no right to take," she went on. "There was no way to make things go back to the way they were. I was hurt, and I was so incredibly sad. But most of all, I was angry. I wanted to hurt him the way he had hurt me. So I took one of his pistols from the closet he kept them in."

Archer was suddenly not so sure he wanted to hear this. But she was lost in her own story; her eyes had taken on a glassy look as she spoke and he had a feeling there would be no stopping her now.

"I waited until he was asleep one night and crept into the bedroom. Everything was shadowy inside, and it was difficult to see. But I made it to the bed without waking him. I knelt down beside him and pointed the gun at his head. I sat that way for a few moments, afraid to go through with it. I kept thinking about what would happen to me when I died, if you can believe that. I was afraid I would go to Hell. The hatred was still in my heart, but I just couldn't do it. I couldn't murder anyone, not even Dean."

Archer sat on the cold ground beside the rock and looked up at her with wide eyes. "What happened?"

"Well, I wasn't the only one with a gun. Dean had gone to bed with one of his pistols; I assume with the intention of shooting me when I came in to go to sleep. He'd had enough of me, I suppose, and all the bourbon he drank didn't help his judgment. When I pressed the gun to his head he woke up and aimed his own gun at me, but I couldn't see it in the darkness. He shot me in the stomach, twice. Unfortunately for him, his gun backfired on the second shot and killed him instantly."

"My god," Archer breathed. "Christina...I don't know what to say. I'm so sorry."

She looked down at him and he saw that although she was crying, her eyes had lost that unfocused, cloudy look they had taken on. He was glad for it. "No need for you to be sorry, dear. What's done is done. It's my own fault I'm stuck here with him forever and not in Heaven with my baby. If I hadn't had murder in my heart, things would be different."

"Why didn't you tell me any of this before? It's horrible that you've had to carry this story around with you all these years," Archer said.

"You were just a boy," Christina said simply. "I couldn't unburden myself to you back then. Besides, just being your friend was enough. The first time I saw you, I knew you were special. You draw displaced spirits to you, did you know that?"

He frowned. "I never really thought about it, but I guess it is strange that I was the only one who could see you and Dean when I was younger. I remember my mother sitting down at the kitchen table right next to you once and never noticing you were there."

"That's because you have a gift. There's something about you, Archer, that attracts the dead. You can see us, hear us. It may be a curse rather than a blessing if you're in the wrong place, I suppose."

He remembered what Dean had said before, about his

motives for "bothering" Archer...because he was being seen and heard and felt, and he liked it.

"There's something important that you need to realize," Christina said, reaching out to gently stroke Archer's face. There was something motherly in the gesture, and he realized that she had probably become so attached to him over the years because she thought of him as the child she lost.

"What is it?" he asked.

"You believe you are dreaming right now, but you aren't....not exactly. This conversation--and the one you had with Dean earlier--is very real. This is the way we communicate with you now, because you are so far away from home."

"I don't understand," he said, but he thought maybe he did, and the idea scared him more than he was willing to admit.

"We still need you, Archer. When I said you were special, I was speaking the truth. It's not everyone who can communicate with the dead in their dreams."

He stood up and took a deep breath, trying to process everything he had just heard. And it did seem as though he had dreamed of the two of them before, that Christina had come to him while he was asleep, but he couldn't remember when or what had been said.

Christina took his arm gently, turning him to face her.

"I don't want to scare you, but you need to know these things. And there's something else...something I've felt since I first sat down here today." She took both his hands in hers and looked into his eyes earnestly. "As a spirit, I can sense when another like me is near. It's a useful tool when someone like Dean is around, that's for sure. Archer, you have another spirit close to you in your world. I can sense her right now. She's there even as we speak."

"What do you mean? Who is she?"

"I have no idea. I hear the name Lucy in my head. Does that name mean anything to you?"

He thought for a moment, then shook his head. "Lucy," he repeated, and his true self said the word along with him as

Lucy Garside looked on at his bedside. "No, nothing comes to mind."

"Just be careful, will you please? Not all spirits are like me. Some of them have an agenda, and they won't rest until it is fulfilled."

Archer felt dizzy with knowledge, breathless with everything he had just learned, as though he had just been punched in the solar plexus. It was almost too much to take in, let alone believe...he wasn't even sure yet that all of this wasn't a dream, just something his overworked brain had cooked up in a fit of exhaustion.

Suddenly, Christina whipped her head around to face the barn, eyes filled with terror. Her hands squeezed his for the barest of moments before letting go as she stepped away from him.

"I have to go. Dean is coming."

"Wait, how will I find you again? To make sure you're okay?"

"I'll be fine. But don't worry, I'll find you. Now go! Before he arrives and finds us together! And Archer?"

He turned to face her one last time.

She bit her lip nervously. "Remember, if I can sense this Lucy person, he can too."

He didn't have to ask who she meant. Dean would be all too happy to interfere, he knew, and even though he hadn't the foggiest of ideas who Lucy was, he felt an odd tingle in his chest at the mention of her name. It made him sure that whoever she turned out to be, he didn't want Dean within a hundred thousand miles of her.

"Thank you, Christina," he said softly.

She smiled at him, and for the briefest of moments he considered staying with her to make sure she would be alright. But then she held up her hand, palm out, so that he could see an odd design drawn there. It looked like an Egyptian hieroglyph, the one that was an eye lined in kohl.

"Wake up," she whispered.

Archer opened his eyes slowly. His bedroom looked the same, but everything had changed at the same time. His head ached with the weight of everything he had just learned, and when he remembered Christina's last words to him he sat up, looking carefully around his room.

There, in the corner, was a girl.

She was writing furiously in some sort of notebook and didn't appear to notice him, so he watched her for a moment. She was beautiful, he saw that right away, but he could tell by the way she was dressed that she was not one of the living; her clothing had an old fashioned appeal to it that bespoke the decade she had lived in rather than a vintage sensibility. Her hair cascaded down her back in loose, dark curls, one of which fell across her cheek as she bent over her notebook. As she lifted her hand to push it back, he saw the faint glimmer of something rainbow-colored above her head. It shimmered like a mirage for a moment and then disappeared, but he had time to realize that it was perhaps the most gorgeous and awesome thing he had ever witnessed; it was as though the aurora borealis had just appeared on his ceiling.

Suddenly, she looked up, right at him. They locked eyes for the barest of moments, and in that short span of time he had two thoughts cross his mind: one, that this could possibly be the girl who had snuck into his hotel room; and two, he would-- without a doubt--do everything in his power to protect her. The dream he had been having was wiped clean from his mind as he looked at her; he didn't remember Christina's warning at all. Yet instinctively, he knew not to be wary of this dead girl. He felt only curiosity and a calm sort of surprise.

"Hello," he said hoarsely.

Chapter Four
Darcy

There was nothing creepier, nothing more guaranteed to give you nightmares, than being alone in a morgue at night.

Darcy was finding this out the hard way.

She had gone to Mercy's house at eight o'clock as they had arranged, wearing all black (at Mercy's suggestion, although Darcy didn't see how it mattered one way or another; she would be invisible the entire time she was at the morgue) and carrying only her cell phone, which she carefully set to the silent ringer. Her hands were steady as she took the potion from Mercy, ominous as it looked; it had been swathed in bubble wrap and placed in a thick canvas bag to keep both it and Darcy protected. Darcy had not a trace of nerves, no sour stomach; she simply had a job to carry out, for which the reward would be handsome.

"Go over with me one more time what you're going to do," Mercy said as she handed over the potion.

"I'll drink the invisibility potion in my car, park on Elm, then walk over to Sycamore. The morgue is in the basement of the funeral home and doesn't have it's own entrance. I'll use your key to get into the outer door, and once I'm inside I'll have to use a magnetic card on a keypad next to the double doors," Darcy recited. She knew the plan by heart, as Mercy had insisted on going over it fifty billion times, as though Darcy was a child. "Speaking of which, how did you get these keys, anyway?"

"Nevermind," Mercy said with a frown. "The less you know, the better. What will you do after you get through the double doors?"

Darcy sighed. "I take the stairs down to basement level and choose the body that's been there the shortest amount of time. Then I unwrap the potion--"

"*Carefully*, don't forget that part," Mercy interrupted. "If you should spill even one drop on yourself--"

"I know, I know! Stop interrupting! Anyway, I *carefully* unwrap the bottle and place two drops on the corpse's tongue. And when he--or she--wakes up, I'm supposed to tell them your name and address."

"And then what?"

"Then I hightail it out of there and bring the bottle and keys back to you."

Mercy looked into her eyes for a moment, searching. Then she sighed and handed over a large brass key, a plastic rectangle about the size of a credit card with a magnetic strip on the back, and the vial of liquid that would make Darcy invisible.

"I hope I'm doing the right thing, trusting you with this," she said. "If anything goes wrong, and I mean *anything*, you abort the plan and get back here as fast as you can. Do you understand?"

Darcy nodded, pocketing the items. "No worries. I'll be back in two shakes."

Mercy watched her bounce down the front steps and into her car with a concerned expression on her face. She knew Darcy was smart and capable, but this job had no room for error.

On the other hand, she thought, if the girl did succeed, Mercy was that much closer to being a millionaire. Perhaps even a billionaire. More importantly, she would have created dozens of allies, people who had been pulled from Death's arms by her magical elixir...and they would be in her debt. She would finally have the power she had dreamed of since discovering she had the ability to speak to those who had passed over; she would rule her own kingdom of the undead. She would be untouchable.

Of course, this wouldn't be the first time she'd dabbled in potions and the dead. But this time would be a success. It had to be. There was no room for failure.

A slow smile had spread across her face.

Now, at the same moment that Archer and Lucy were meeting for the first time, Darcy crept down the shadowed hallways of the funeral home until she found a door marked "Stairs". It was unlocked, and she pushed it open slowly. If there was a security camera in the vicinity, the recording would show the door moving on its own, perhaps swept open by the force of the furnace kicking on in the basement. It was an old building, one of the oldest in town, and surely not all the floors were level; certainly the doors didn't sit flush in their frames anymore. This would be the reasoning of anyone who happened to see the security footage, Darcy thought. No one would guess in a million years that the door had been opened by an invisible girl.

The stairwell was spooky, dimly lit as it was, and Darcy hurried to get to her destination. The irony that she was hurrying towards a room full of dead people was not lost on her; she was no dummy.

When she reached the bottom of the stairs, she immediately saw a dim blue light to her left and stopped in her tracks, suddenly sure she was not alone. What if one of the morticians was still here, working late? She only had one hour of guaranteed invisible time from the small dose of potion she'd taken, and it had already been at least fifteen minutes since she had ingested it. She waited where she was for a moment, then stepped cautiously into a shadowy corner of the room.

It was empty. At least, it was empty of living people, she thought, and shivered. The blue light came from a small clock mounted on the wall which was encircled in neon.

She had imagined something much different from what was before her; having only seen the inside of a morgue in movies and on television, she had expected a cold, sterile room with metal slabs and lots of scientific-looking equipment. But this room looked much like any other finished basement she had ever been in, right down to the dark wood paneling on the walls. There were large, floor-to-ceiling cabinets to her right;

on her left sat a big old relic of a desk, the kind with a tan metal base which looked exactly like the ones elementary school teachers used. An extremely old desktop computer sat there, and judging by its size Darcy guessed it was roughly twenty years old.

The only things that gave the room away for what it was were the tile floor--sloped at a slight angle towards a large round drain in the middle--and a small cluster of machinery that stood in a corner. These had dials and readout windows and lengths of rubber tubing attached, and Darcy assumed these were for pumping the blood out of the bodies and sending in the formaldehyde.

The long cabinets seemed to be her best bet for finding a body. Before moving toward them, she scanned the room for security cameras, almost positive she wouldn't find one. The funeral home, which was the only one in their small town, was operated by two brothers, Bill and Nelson Whitaker. They were well known for being extremely tight-fisted, and Darcy couldn't imagine them shelling out the dough for a camera when their computer was so hideously outdated. Unless it was hidden behind a wall, there was no telltale gleam from a lens or flashing red light to indicate something was recording the goings-on inside the morgue. If there had been, a small pair of pliers in Darcy's back pocket would have taken care of it. She was quite handy with technical things, and had come prepared.

The cabinets weren't locked, which sort of came as a surprise. She hadn't expected this to be so easy, even though Mercy had assured her it would be. Although, she reminded herself, she hadn't even come to the hard part yet.

The first cabinet was empty save for a long, stainless steel tray. Darcy let out a breath she hadn't even realized she'd been holding and closed the door gently, moving on to the next one. It, too, was empty. The third cabinet, however, had an occupant.

The body was covered in a thin white sheet, so she couldn't tell if it was a man or a woman. Not that it mattered, she supposed...but if she really wanted to be honest with herself, seeing the dead body of a woman would remind her too much of finding her mother, and that was a memory she tried to keep repressed as much as possible.

She steadied herself by thinking of Archer. She would see him soon, and that thought made her exquisitely happy. She had been working on a plan to bump into him at his favorite coffee shop, even writing a script of sorts so that when she started a conversation with him she wouldn't be at a loss for words. She knew he was a small town boy, and they had that in common. She also knew that he wasn't fond of all the attention he had been getting lately; he was really a shy person at heart, she thought with a little smile. He had never come right out and said he hated his fame, but she could see the discomfort on his face when he had to attend red carpet events and the flashbulbs went off all around him. He couldn't go anywhere without a mob of screaming girls following him. She didn't want to be just another one of those girls....

Maybe being the one girl who had never heard of him was the route she should take, she thought suddenly. What an inspired idea!

And just like that, out of nowhere, came a memory she usually repressed. That was the sneaky thing with memories, she thought distantly; they could creep up on you when your mind was otherwise occupied and attack, regardless of how long you'd been keeping it buried.

It wasn't as though she was scared of the memory, or ashamed of it; well, not completely. It just represented a time in her life she felt it was best to forget. Sometimes, she thought, when you are forced to do something which might be considered amoral or illegal, it's better to move on in an effort to put a distance between yourself and that thing. She had discovered that putting certain things out of her head lessened the chances that others would think about it again, and that was good. Especially in her hometown.

*****

Darcy had obtained a fake ID when she was eighteen, after pestering her best friend's older sister to hand over her old driver's license. Michelle Hicks looked quite a bit like Darcy, if the lighting was right and the person who was looking didn't look too closely. Of course, Darcy learned early on that if a guy was working the door to a club, all she had to do was flash the card and a little thigh to gain entrance. Men were so easy.

The reason she wanted the ID was simple: she'd discovered a local band, an alt-country group called Four On The Floor, and the lead singer was delicious. He had everything Darcy looked for in a guy--a hard look, stage presence, the sense that perhaps he could be a little mean when he didn't get his way-- and best of all, he was on his way to being famous. The band was attracting major attention from Nashville and from other, bigger bands, who were tapping their services as an opening act left and right. When they played a bar within driving distance, Darcy made it her business to be there. There was something about the singer--James Keith--that was impossible for her to get out of her mind. And though she'd had celebrity crushes before, she knew this was different. At every show, she made an effort to get right down in front, right where he would see her as he leaned into the microphone, his shirt sleeves rolled up so as not to get in the way when he played guitar. And he always looked at her, making eye contact for the barest of moments before sliding his gaze away indifferently. She knew he had to do that in order to keep up appearances; it was the same thing as a big star not letting on that he had a girlfriend. It alienated female fans, that was all.

When she thought back to the crushes she'd had on movie stars or musicians during her early teen years, she could only laugh. Back then, the word "love" had meant something to her; back then, she had imagined she was in love with boys she'd never even met, had never even been in the same room with. Once, after seeing a favorite childhood television star in his first film, she had watched with dismay, horror, and finally anger as he kissed his co-star passionately. It seemed to go on forever, and by the time the movie was over, she felt sick to her stomach. She'd gone home immediately and ripped all his posters off the walls of her bedroom, infuriated that he would do such a thing when he knew he owed an enormous debt to his female audience. And afterward, she'd looked at the mess on her floor, posters and centerfolds from teen magazines torn to shreds and her hands bleeding from twenty different paper cuts, and she thought she might feel sorry, but she didn't. It was what he deserved for never responding to her fan letters, for letting her down, for daring to make out with some unknown girl on a movie screen.

But over time, her anger had seemed to fade until it became a silly childhood memory. After a year or so, she no longer even thought the actor was cute; he had simply been something to occupy her attention before she was mature enough to find a real boy to bestow her love upon.

The boys she went to school with wouldn't do, however. They were all too self-absorbed, too immature, to appreciate her. She would watch them in the cafeteria, messing around and making jokes at the expense of one another, throwing food, shooting spitballs at random people as they passed by, and deem them unworthy of her attentions. She didn't have the patience.

So she had waited, and just when it seemed like she would be alone forever, she had gone to a club on a whim the first time Four On The Floor played her hometown. From that night on, she was hooked. She had known James was the guy for her; his songs touched a chord in her that had never been strummed, and she could see a look in his eyes that matched one she recognized in her own. It was a look of longing, of pain, of being hurt over and over and needing someone to fill up an empty space in the heart.

After several shows, she finally worked up the courage to talk to him one night at Redmon's, a tiny bar tucked away inside a stand of trees so dense you had to know exactly where the building was to find it. The club did a good business, mostly with country fans and the few college kids who knew about it. To them, it was a good place to get away, a sort of secret hideout which held the same attraction a treehouse might to a kid.

He was sitting at a table by himself after the performance, his shirt soaked in sweat, nursing a beer. His bandmates had disappeared out back, probably to smoke and flirt with the endless stream of girls waiting to gush over them. The bar had emptied out quickly after the band left the stage; there was another local band playing across town and they always drew a crowd. Darcy made her way to the table and sat down across from him rather boldly, knowing if she didn't make a move then she would regret it.

"Hey," she said softly.

"Hey, yourself," he replied, turning the beer bottle in lazy circles on the table. There were several damp rings there, left by other bottles, and she wondered how many he'd had.

"I just wanted to thank you for your music", she said. "I come to all your shows, and when I leave I always feel a little better than when I came in."

He looked up at her sharply, as though trying to determine whether or not she was making fun of him, and decided she was being genuine.

"Thank you," he said, his hands finally becoming still. The bottle was empty, she saw, and he pushed it aside. His dark eyes were relentless, probing her own before moving down. "I appreciate that. What's your name?"

"Darcy," she breathed, and felt her cheeks get hot. The way he was looking at her was the way a hungry man might look at a large plate of warm food.

"Darcy," he repeated, rolling the name around on his tongue. "I'm James."

She tucked her hair behind her ear nervously, realizing her legs were numb from the knees down. The combination of his voice and her name was enough to send her reeling. She wanted very badly to reach across the table and touch his face, feel the stubble beneath her fingers, but didn't dare.

He smiled suddenly, for the first time all night, and she returned it with fervor, feeling a little butterfly of panic making waves in her stomach. She had practiced her first encounter with him a hundred times in her head, getting it just right, but she hadn't counted on him being so...intense. And now that they had spoken, she didn't know where things would go from here.

"Hey, there you are," said a silky voice from behind her, and all at once she realized what he had been smiling at. She turned slowly, so slowly she thought she might hear the tendons in her neck creak, and saw a tall, slender girl standing behind her. She was pretty in the way country girls sometimes were, with smooth tanned skin and no makeup. Her long, dyed red hair hung halfway down her back.

"Just takin' a break before the guys come back in," he said to the girl, ignoring Darcy. She felt a sudden and inexplicable rage come over her, directed at this redhead who had ruined the moment she'd taken pains to construct. And she was wearing cutoffs, Darcy saw with distaste, smirking. What trash.

"You wanna go for a walk with me?" the girl asked him,

and the casual way she said it clicked a certainty into place in Darcy's mind. She was his girlfriend, then. Not just some random bar groupie but his actual girlfriend. Darcy shuddered and stood up far too quickly, scooting the metal chair back on the concrete floor so that it made a shrieking sound.

"I've gotta go," she said tersely. "See ya."

She turned and fled, not waiting for a response, not waiting to see if the redhead was looking after her with a curious expression on her face. She walked quickly to the door, throwing it open and sucking in the cool air that had come in after midnight, feeling the heat in her cheeks even more against the chill of the night. She didn't think, couldn't think, about what had just happened. She allowed her mind to go blank and looked up at the stars winking at her from their place in the inky heavens.

It didn't come to her until later, what she had to do. When it did come, she was lying in bed, consumed with the memory of James' strong hand on the beer bottle, with thoughts of how his eyes had looked as they roved over her hungrily. She was about to drift off when the image of water came to her, the muddy water of the Mississippi. She saw it rushing in her mind's eye, moving toward the horizon, and suddenly, just like that, she had an answer. A way to take care of the redheaded girl.

*****

She had been standing in front of the open cabinet during her daydream about James and suddenly she saw a white rectangle in her peripheral vision. Turning towards it, she realized it was an I.D. tag that had been placed on the inside of the cabinet door. She leaned down for a better look.

"Jason Matthew Lewis," Darcy read aloud. She scanned the rest of the card, reading the last bit of information anyone would ever need to know about him: he was forty-seven, his date of birth was June 10, and he had died the day before of a heart attack. A quick check of the remaining two cabinets told her they were empty, as she had thought they might be. Unless there's a tragic accident, small towns rarely have full morgues.

"Well, Jason Lewis, you'll do," Darcy said, and pulled the stainless steel table towards her.

Chapter Five
Archer and Lucy

She sat very still at the small dining room table, watching him as he busied himself in the kitchen. The floor plan of his apartment was open, so she could sit in one spot and still see him as he moved from place to place. A long counter separated the kitchen--which was adjacent to the dining area--from the living room. She was impressed by his humble home; it was far from the palatial mansion she had envisioned before arriving.

After the initial shock of realizing that Archer could see and hear her had begun to fade, Lucy found she didn't know what to say to him. She had pictured meeting him a thousand times, scripted their conversations in her head, but now that the time was actually here, her tongue and brain didn't seem to want to work together. It seemed he wasn't entirely sure where to begin either, as he was moving from cabinet to cabinet, unsure of where certain items were in his own kitchen. She'd assured him she didn't need to eat or drink but he insisted on making coffee anyway. Something about the ritual of it calmed his nerves, she sensed.

"How long have you been here?" he asked over his shoulder. He was pouring coffee grounds into the machine on the counter--their scent was heavenly--and she watched his back, the way his shoulder blades moved beneath the thin t-shirt he wore. He turned to her then and she quickly looked away with heat in her cheeks, as though he had caught her in some shameful act.

"I've lived in New York my whole life," she said softly, not daring to meet his eyes.

"No, I meant, how long have you been in my apartment?" he clarified with the slightest hint of a smile.

"Oh. Of course, how silly of me. Well, let's see....only since you got back into town. And I left when you were showering, I swear!" she added hastily, as though he had accused her of something. "I mean...I wouldn't intrude on something so private."

Archer came to the table and sat down across from her. "I appreciate that. Although I'm wondering why I didn't see you until I woke up if you've been here for..." He consulted his watch. "Ten hours, give or take?"

"Oh, I never came out into the open until you were asleep. Mostly I stayed in the hallway, or in the shadowy space at the back of your closet."

"Why would you hide if you didn't know I could see you?" he asked, confused. Was it possible she *was* the girl who had snuck into his hotel room?

Lucy appeared genuinely at a loss for an answer. "I can't explain it, really. I suppose I was just afraid to get too close to you for the very same reason I'm here: from the moment I saw you on screen at the Imperial Theater, I felt I needed to find you. I still don't know why, but the feeling was too strong to ignore. So strong that I left the place I've called home for over seventy-five years with only my journal, something I've never done. I have never felt anything like this. It...scares me a little."

"How did you know where to find me?"

This was something she was almost ashamed to admit, because the answer made her sound like a stalker. But something in his dark eyes told her that she must be truthful.

"I waited for you at the airport and heard you tell the cabbie your address."

He nodded slowly. "I wouldn't have noticed you at the airport, I was too busy trying to get out of there without causing a scene."

"I'm sorry I've invaded your privacy," Lucy said, and Archer could hear genuine regret in her voice. It touched him. "It's not something I would have done if I felt I had a choice."

"No harm done," he said, and when she looked up at him he saw relief in her eyes. "But I have to know something. May I see your wrists?"

She gave him a puzzled look. "My wrists?"

"Please."

He held his hands out to her, palms up, and she slowly

raised her own and laid them inside his. They looked extraordinarily small and fragile in his large palms, and when he touched her he found that the surface of her skin was soft, yet...insubstantial, like something that might go away if he breathed too hard. Nevertheless, he turned her wrists over gently so he could examine the pale skin on the inside, and found them free of tattoos. Not that he had really expected to find anything.

"I don't think I even need to ask, but you weren't in my hotel room in London yesterday, were you?"

"No. It's difficult for me to travel outside of New York."

"I see. Well, it was worth a shot. I didn't really believe it was you, anyway."

She tilted her head and gave him a confused look. "You didn't believe what was me?"

"When I was in London for the opening of *Look West*--my latest movie--I had an intruder break into my hotel room somehow. She took pictures of me while I was asleep and then left them there so I would know she had been there. She also left one of her, but her face wasn't visible. Just long dark hair and a pink tattoo of my initials on her wrist."

"Oh my goodness!" she cried, bringing her hand up to her mouth. "That is so scary! Well, I promise, it wasn't me. I could never intrude on someone's privacy that way," she said, shaking her head.

He searched her face for any sign that she was lying--her lack of tattoos was reassuring, but didn't necessarily clear her name--but found none. Besides, he wanted to believe her; she seemed earnest in a way that was refreshing. She refused to meet his eyes, but he thought that was simply due to the fact that she was in the same room with a living man who could see her...a man she had a crush on, if he was reading those blushes correctly.

They shared a moment of comfortable silence and when she dared to look up she saw he was watching her intently, but with no sign of fear or discomfort. It was odd, really, that he hadn't been shocked to find a dead girl in his apartment.

"You sure are taking all this with ease," she said. "It's not every man who wakes up to find a dead girl in his home and then makes her coffee."

He smiled. "I hate to spout cliches, but I honestly feel like I've known you for a long time. I think maybe I dreamed about you before we met."

"Really? Has that ever happened to you before?"

"Not that I recall. But my mind is a strange place. I never know what it's going to throw at me next."

She smiled at that and then looked down at her hands. "Can I ask you something?"

"Of course. Ask me anything."

"How long have you been able to see the dead?"

"Since I was a child," he answered, and got up to pour himself a cup of coffee. "I grew up on a twenty-acre farm in North Carolina and there were two spirits there, Dean and Christina. They were husband and wife. Christina was always nice to me. Her husband..." He paused, suddenly recalling the dreams he'd had earlier in the day. Hadn't Dean said something about Archer's dad? Some off-hand remark that had made Archer want to punch him, only he wasn't quite sure what it was now. It was like having a word on the tip of your tongue and not being able to retrieve it. "Not so much," he finished, and brought his coffee to the table.

She looked up at him then, her pallid face expressing curiosity and sadness. "Have you seen others since then?"

He sipped his coffee and pondered the question. There had been his father, but he wasn't ready to talk about that yet. Not even with Lucy.

"Not really. I have dreams, though...very realistic dreams."

She nodded. "You talked a bit in your sleep earlier. It wasn't anything I could make out, really, just the sort of sleep gibberish we all speak at one time or another. But I did hear you say my name."

He looked up sharply at that. "Your name?"

"Yes," she said with a little laugh. "Well, you said, "Lucy". I'm sure it wasn't me you were referring to."

Amanda Crum

"I'm not so sure," he said, peering into the depths of his coffee. Her words had caused a riot in his brain, but nothing formed a cohesive thought; it was all a jumbled mess. Something to do with Christina...

"I don't know anyone named Lucy except you," he explained after a moment.

"Oh," she said with a little frown. "But how...?"

She didn't have to finish the thought. It was the same one going through Archer's head.

"I don't know. But it does seem that we were meant to meet, you and I," he said.

Lucy felt a flush in her cheeks again and looked down at the table, her fingers tracing a pattern on the wood.

"Listen," she said, "I don't pretend to know everything about how all this works, even though I've been dead for a long time. Most things are still a mystery to me, like why some spirits go to one place and some go to another...but I have learned to trust my instincts over the years. And right now they're telling me that I am supposed to know you. If you don't feel the same way...if my being here causes you discomfort, I will leave right now and you will never see me again. I don't want to be the cause of any pain to you, Archer."

It was the first time she had said his name in his presence, and he started at the sound of it. He hadn't heard a female speak to him with such sweetness and honesty since the last time he spoke to his mother.

"I don't want you to leave," he said immediately. "I don't know much right now, but that I'm sure of."

He looked into her pale eyes, and she looked into his dark ones, and there was a moment between them that Archer had only ever read about in books. It was the sort of heart-stopping, time-slowing moment that seemed more like a dream than anything else, and in Lucy's eyes he saw the purest form of love and honesty there is. It was unlike anything he had ever encountered in a living human being.

"Tell me about yourself," he said with a smile, and the one she returned was so bright it made him think of clouds breaking away from the sun.

****

They talked for hours, until the sun came up over the city. Archer realized, at three in the morning, that he hadn't eaten all day when his stomach began rumbling. He barely felt the hunger pangs; he knew nothing but the startling blue color of Lucy's eyes as she listened intently to his stories of growing up in the south. He told her about his family and his love for the land they had lived on when he was young, and when it was her turn to talk he knew nothing but the sound of her voice and the memories she shared. She talked about her family and Benjamin, the house she had grown up in, and what New York had looked like when she was alive. And when her story led to the day she died, she couldn't help but shed a tear at the memories that came flooding back with it. The passing years hadn't diminished her sadness, he saw, and reached across the table to take her hand. She froze for a moment at the unexpected touch, but didn't shy away. He was again struck by the odd feeling of her skin; it was like grasping something made of silk.

"I'm sorry to be so emotional," she said, toying with her locket It was a nervous habit she hadn't outgrown from childhood. "But Ben was my best friend, and I still carry a burden of guilt for how we left things. He...he was in love with me, but I was too selfish to love him back. I couldn't give him what he needed, and then he was forced to watch me die."

"I don't think you were selfish at all," Archer said softly. "And don't ever apologize. You can't create feelings of love if they aren't already there. It wouldn't have been fair to him *or* you."

She smiled a sad little smile. "I suppose you're right. It's just so hard to tell myself that when I know what happened to him after I died; he hung himself. And even though I've stayed pretty close to my old neighborhood since I died, I've never seen him. I have no idea where he went. My friend Irish says

103

that the afterlife is different for all of us, that some spirits stay here and some go...somewhere else. No one knows for sure, and no one knows why we don't all end up together. It's all very confusing. I just wish I could see him one more time, to tell him I'm sorry."

"If he's the sort of fellow you say he is, I doubt he would be expecting an apology from you," Archer said.

She gave him an appreciative smile, and there was a moment of comfortable silence between them. She loved the way he spoke; softly, but with confidence, and with the drawling accent that had followed him from North Carolina.

"Why do you think I'm here?" she asked finally. "I mean, have you had other spirits tell you they were drawn to you?"

He thought about it for a moment. A snippet of his dream had come back to him...Christina had said that he was special, that spirits came to him to be heard. Yet Lucy was the first one to approach him since he was a child...why was that?

"The woman I told you about, Christina...she told me that because I can see and hear the dead, they would come to me for help. But you're the first one I've ever known, other than her and her husband."

"Maybe they come to you in dreams," Lucy said off-handedly. She was still reeling from the touch of his hand on hers and wasn't really aware of much else.

But her words struck a chord in him, and although he still didn't remember most of his dreams, he had a feeling that what she said was true. There were always haunting images that never quite merged together after he woke up, and there was the feeling that something important had just happened that he had no memory of. It made sense.

"I think you're right," he said, and got up to refill his coffee cup. He had to take his hand away in order to do so, and Lucy almost sighed at the loss. "So, what does that mean to you? Do you need my help?"

"I don't know yet," Lucy replied honestly.

And in the coming days, the two of them would find that it was very nearly the other way around.

Ghosts of the Imperial

Chapter Six

Front page article from the New York Star:

Hotel Maid Confesses Her Key Card Was Stolen On Night of Archer's Break-In!

It seems Archer Black's team of security guards was unable to keep an overzealous fan out of his room at The Four Seasons London, according to an unnamed source. It happened early last week while he was in town to promote his latest movie, Look West.

"No one saw this coming," says Victor Cross, manager of The Four Seasons. "I assure you that all the necessary steps were taken to track down the perpetrator, but he or she has vanished into thin air. My security staff are at a loss."

Hotel officials say a fan apparently broke into Mr. Black's penthouse suite while he was asleep, then left a package for him at the front desk...all while the security cameras were rolling. It was unclear how anyone could have gotten into the star's room until Dolores Crenshaw, head chambermaid for TFS, broke down and admitted yesterday that her key card had been stolen the day of the break-in.

"I had it at six o'clock when I did my rounds," a teary Miss Crenshaw said, "But when I went to clock out for the night I realized it wasn't in my pocket anymore. I just don't know how it could have fallen out, the pockets on our uniforms are too deep. I think someone must have stolen it somehow."

As most people who have stayed at a modern hotel know, the doors to all the rooms are opened by an electronic key card instead of by an actual key. At The Four Seasons, only the chambermaids and the hotel manager have access to all of the rooms by way of a master key card, but the penthouse suite is opened by it's own, separate key card.

When asked why she hadn't come forward with this

information right away, Miss Crenshaw would only say that she was afraid she would lose her job. As for how someone got up to the penthouse floor without being seen on camera, the hotel staff had no comment at press time.

****

Archer had insisted on Lucy sleeping in his bed, even though she assured him she didn't need to rest. He made it up with clean sheets for her and then sat in the leather chair she had occupied earlier. He was tired, but he wasn't anxious to jump back into the dreams he'd been having, even if it meant he got to see Christina again. That last dream still troubled him, mostly because he felt like something very important had been given to him and he had lost it. Also, he was more than curious about the symbol that had been drawn on Christina's hand. He wondered if she controlling his dreams somehow.

"I can't tell you the last time I slept in a bed," Lucy said, and he couldn't miss the sadness in her voice. "It's been a very long time."

"You said you don't need to rest, but you *can* sleep, right? I mean, you sleep like we do."

As soon as the words were out of his mouth, he regretted them. The look on her face was almost an expression of agony. It hurt his heart more than he thought possible. But she didn't let on that his words had hurt her.

"I can sleep, yes," she said, and managed a weak smile. "Although it's been so long since I rested like the living that I'm no longer sure they're one and the same. Maybe the dreams are different. They certainly seem more real."

"Mine are pretty realistic, too. I think maybe you hit the nail on the head when you said the dead are communicating with me while I sleep. I can't remember, though...once I wake up, there is only a vague memory there, and I go through the day like a zombie, trying to recall what was said or what happened. It's like having a bit of a song stuck in your head and you think you know what it is, but you can't quite get it. It's

107

enough to drive a person mad."

She was nodding enthusiastically. "I know just what you mean! Sometimes I dream of things that don't quite make sense, and there is always the feeling that it *would* make sense, if I just thought about it hard enough."

He nodded, very familiar with that feeling.

"Right after I died, I sat in the theater--The Imperial--for a long time. I think I slept then...I can't remember, exactly. I kept thinking of my family, and what would become of Ben after what he'd witnessed, but I also thought of silly things, like the fact that I would never taste warm chocolate chip cookies again or feel a breeze on my face. I had only been gone for a matter of hours, I suppose, but I knew those things instinctively. And they hurt my heart. I never thought a person could hurt that much and come out okay on the other side of things. But I suppose I did. When you take away everyone a girl loves and everything that gives her comfort, when you take away her humanity, all that is left is her will to go on."

Archer watched her as she spoke, the way her lovely face was set as she talked of being strong, and he felt himself falling in love with her. It was inescapable and total and crushing, that feeling.

He didn't plan what he did next; it came to him as naturally as breathing.

She looked up at him, not in surprise, but as though to ask him if it was really okay. He didn't speak, didn't need to. She stood from the bed in one fluid motion and fell into his arms, and this time he didn't notice the odd, silken effect of her skin at all. She was immediately astonished at the feel of him; he was the first human she had touched--really touched, and not just brushed up against--since becoming a spirit, and had she been alive, it would have taken her breath away. His chest was massive and thick with muscle, something she wouldn't have guessed just by looking at him. His arms felt like two steel vise grips around her waist, and she felt a small shiver go through her at the contact. It was wonderful, this feeling. She felt safe. Finally, after all these years of being alone, she felt safe.

Archer wound his arms around her and rested his cheek on top of her head. For a moment, he wasn't worried with anything else in the world; not his ailing mother, his career, or his agent. All he knew was the insubstantial weight of her against him and the clean scent of her hair and the way she seemed at ease for the first time since she had arrived. It was wonderful.

****

Archer awoke to the burring of his cell phone and nearly fell out of the chair he had crashed in. Every shade had been drawn in his bedroom, but the sunlight still managed to creep in through minute cracks in the blinds. He snagged a glance at his alarm clock and was astonished to see that it was three o'clock in the afternoon. *We nearly slept the day away*, he thought, and on the heels of that thought was another, clearer one: *Where is Lucy?*

His bed was empty and neatly made. There was no sign that anyone had been in his room other than him, and for some reason that made him uneasy. But before he could go investigate, his phone made its insistent little buzz again and he picked it up, rubbing a hand across his eyes.

"Hello?"

"Hey baby, it's Mama."

"Hey Mama!" he said, waking up a little more. "How are you feeling?"

"Better, much better. How are things in the big city?"

You wouldn't believe me if I told you, he thought. "Things are good, Mama. I just got back from London. The new movie is getting some real good reviews there."

"I bet," she said with a smile in her voice. "I know it will do great no matter where it opens. I am so proud of you, baby."

"Thank you, Mama. That means a lot to me."

Just then, he heard another woman's voice in the background, but he couldn't make out who it was or what she was saying. There was a muffled sound as his mama put her hand over the mouthpiece of the phone, and then he heard her

109

say, "I will, woman, you hush!" When she came back on she was laughing. "June says to tell you she always knew you would be a big star, and you better thank her in your Oscar speech."

June was June Goodman, a good friend of his mama's who visited at least three times a week to make sure she had everything she needed; Archer was grateful to her for helping out when he was away.

"Tell her I'll do her one better, I'll invite you and her as my special guests to the awards shows so she can hear me thank her in person."

His mother relayed the message and he heard a shriek of excited laughter in the background, which made him grin.

"Everyone back home says to tell you hi," she went on. "Myra Watkins saw an interview you did on the television and said you are just as handsome as ever. She also said her daughter is single now, just so you know."

He laughed at that and shook his head. "Tell her thanks, but I'm not really lookin' right now."

"Oh? Got a girlfriend, have you?"

He thought for a moment on how to answer that one. *Sure I do, she's been dead for seventy five years but she sure is beautiful.*

"No, Mama," he said quietly. "No girlfriends here."

"I'm just teasin' you," she said playfully, and he smiled. How long had it been since she had sounded so good, so alert? Too long.

"You sound like you're having a good day," he said. "Did the doctor let you try that new medicine he was talking about?"

"No, I'm on the same meds. But I met someone...interesting."

Archer frowned. "A man?"

"No, not a man, don't go getting all protective," she mock-scolded. "A woman. A *psychic* woman, at that."

"A psychic? I thought you didn't believe in that stuff."

"Well, I've opened my mind a little since the big C hit me," she said, and he realized it was the first time his mother had ever alluded to the fact that she had cancer. She had never come right out and said it; she had always danced around the subject, pushing it aside as if it were little more than a head cold.

"How did you meet?"

"She just moved in down the way, in the old Stevenson house. It's been up for sale forever, you know, since Jake Stevenson died, and I guess the realtor must have finally decided to put it up on their website, because the new owner is from Virginia. Anyway, she came over this morning to introduce herself, and one thing led to another and she ended up reading my tarot cards."

"Really?" This didn't sound like his Mama, having her tarot cards read by a stranger. And it certainly was unlike her to invite someone into her home while she was ill.

"Do you know what she told me? She said that I have at least another five years," his mother said jubilantly. "Can you beat that? Five years! That's four years better than what the doc said!"

"Mama, I'm not sure you should put too much stock into what this lady says, you barely know her--"

"I knew you'd say that, darlin', and I know you're only looking out for your old mama, but I really feel like it could be true. I mean, just listen to me! Can't you tell I feel better? I woke up today with a spring in my step that hasn't been there since....well, since your father died, if I want to be honest."

Archer closed his eyes briefly. "You do sound like you feel better. I'm glad, really. I just want you to be happy."

"I know you do, baby. And I love you for it."

"Listen, maybe I should come home for a little while. I don't feel like I'm being a very good son, so many miles away while you're sick."

"Don't you worry about me," she insisted. "I'm fine. I'd feel guilty if you came home because of me and it messed up your schedule. I know you're busy, honey. You stay there and do what you have to do, and I'll be here when you're done."

There was no arguing with her when she was like this, he

Amanda Crum

knew, and so he didn't attempt to protest. It was a decision he would come to regret later.

"Alright, Mama. I'll let you go so you can rest."

"Rest? Hell, I feel like I could run a marathon right now!"

"Don't go overboard," he said with a little laugh. He had to admit, it was good to hear her sound this way again. "I'll call you when I know for sure what my schedule is like for the rest of the month, and then we can work out a visit, okay?"

"Sounds good, honey. You take care."

"You too. I love you, Mama."

"I love you too, son."

He hung up and scrubbed his face with one hand, feeling vaguely hungover. Staying up late didnt agree with him, it seemed. Suddenly he remembered Lucy and got up to investigate the rest of the apartment.

The smell of burnt coffee assaulted his nose when he walked into the kitchen, and he had to smile when he saw Lucy standing at the sink, pouring a batch of foul-smelling liquid down the drain.

"I'm sorry," she said sheepishly. "I thought you'd like some when you woke up, but I don't know how to work this machine."

He walked towards her and gently took the carafe, placing it back on the coffee maker. He pulled her to him and wrapped his arms around her, something that still made her feel weak in the stomach. She didn't know if she would ever get used to the feeling of his strong arms, the warmth he gave off, or the way she felt perfectly safe for the first time in a lot of years.

"I'm glad you stayed last night," he said softly. "Thank you for trusting me with your story."

She pulled back and smiled up at him. "Thank you for listening. Mabye this *is* what you're meant to do...listen to our stories, I mean. You're awfully good at it."

He didn't have to ask who she meant by "our"...but for some reason, he didn't like that she grouped herself in with the spirit world. It was another reminder that he was falling for someone he could never have.

112

"Maybe I should leave Hollywood," he joked. "Focus on my calling."

She smiled then, but it was weak, as if she didn't like him joking about it.

"I'm sorry, I shouldn't be so lighthearted about it," he said immediately. "Maybe you're right, maybe this is what I'm supposed to do."

She didn't respond, just laid her head against his chest and listened to his heartbeat for a moment. It was a comforting sound.

"Why don't I go down the street and get us some coffee?" he said after a moment. "Would you like to stay here again tonight?"

She looked up at him. "I would love to."

A moment later, watching him leave, she wondered if perhaps she should go back to The Imperial. Something was happening between the two of them...and it could only end badly, she thought.

Chapter Seven

Darcy had hurried back to Mercy's house after carrying out her job at the morgue, trying to push away thoughts of what she had just done and seen. It was harder than she had imagined it to be, and as soon as she got to Mercy's street she pulled over to the side of the road and shut off the engine, scared to drive any further. Her legs were shaking uncontrollably.

The dead man had lain there harmlessly enough, she recalled, even after she placed the drops of liquid on his tongue; nothing had happened for more than half a minute. She counted the seconds off on her watch as Mercy had instructed her to do. Then, suddenly, his eyes had popped open and he jerked up on the stainless steel table like a man waking up from a bad dream.

He stared straight ahead for a moment, his pale skin seeming to glow in the faint blue light emanating from the clock. The sheet fell from his chest with a soft slithery sound and landed in a puddle in his lap. His eyes were two steely points of light, silvery in the dimness of the basement.

Darcy stood frozen where she was for a moment, afraid to move. She felt a bit like Mickey Mouse in Fantasia, who had known enough to get the brooms started but not enough to make them stop. She was just about to take a step back and slowly make her way toward the stairs when he spoke.

"Where am I?"

His voice was hoarse and creaky, as though his throat was tight. He turned to Darcy and pierced her with his eyes, eyes that were like two headlights shining in the darkness.

"*Where am I?*" he repeated loudly.

"Th-the morgue," Darcy stuttered. She finally unglued her feet from the basement floor and took a step backward, afraid he might jump off the table at her.

He looked down at himself, holding his hands out in front of him. She could see tiny veins showing blue through his skin, as though it were paper thin. The only sound for several moments was the ticking of the clock.

"I'm dead," he said softly. "I died."

"I'm sorry," Darcy said, nodding. "But...you're not exactly dead anymore."

"What?" He turned to her and she heard the tendons in his neck creak like the hinges on an old door. "What did you say?"

She took another big step back and felt the bottom stair hit the back of her shoe. "I said, you're not exactly dead anymore. Someone sent me here with medicine to bring you back. A friend."

He said nothing, simply sat there looking at her in disbelief. And astonishingly, he began to cry.

"Don't be scared, it's okay," Darcy said, unable to keep a quiver out of her voice. "The woman who made the elixir I gave you...she lives here in town, on Boston Avenue. Her name is Mercy Deveroux. If you find her, she'll help you. That's all she wants; to help."

She turned and made her way up the stairs, listening on the way for the sound of his feet hitting the tile floor. She was halfway up the staircase when he spoke again.

"I was with my wife."

Darcy stopped and turned around, but stayed where she was on the riser.

"What?" she called.

He was sobbing softly. "I was with my wife. She died in a car accident two years ago and...I never thought I would see her again. When I died, I..." He trailed off, and Darcy held her breath for a moment. "I found her," he finished. "I found her and then you brought me back and *you ripped me away from her!*"

That was all Darcy needed to get going again. She stumbled up the remaining six steps and flung open the door, not caring if there was a video camera recording anymore. She could have sworn she'd heard footsteps down below as she put her hand on the door, bare feet slapping cold tile.

She got to the big double doors and fumbled in her pocket for the key card, knowing it wouldn't be there, it would have fallen out of her pocket on the stairs...she would have to go back to the staircase to get it and he would be there, waiting for her with those silver eyes shining in the dark---

But it was there. She wrestled it from her jeans and slid it across the card reader with shaking hands. After a moment, the red light on the reader changed to green and she heard the tumblers in the doors unlock. She shoved the doors open and had a heartstopping moment when she thought she really had lost the key to the outer door; but it was shoved into the small watchpocket in her jeans instead of the bigger one. She yanked it free and a moment later she was breathing in cool fall air.

Darcy stood outside, trying to get her breath, trying to will her knees to stop shaking. After a moment she felt okay enough to walk to her car, but with the image of the dead man still clear in her mind, she ran. She had never heard such anguish in someone's voice, such anger...and she had been the cause of it. Well, Mercy was the actual cause, but Darcy had played her part.

And now, because she had followed Mercy's directions to a T, they were in danger. The dead man knew Mercy's address.

She went from a run to a full sprint and didn't slow down until she got to her car.

****

A little while later she was bursting through Mercy's front door with terror in her eyes, her hair a wild and tangled mess from the wind.

"Mercy! *Mercy*!" she called frantically.

"For Heaven's sake, child, I'm right here!" Mercy said, emerging from the kitchen and wiping her hands on a dish towel. "What's the matter with you?"

"I did what you told me to do and he's mad, Mercy! He's seriously pissed! We have to leave, right now!"

Mercy grasped Darcy by the shoulders and shook her firmly. "Slow down! I can't understand a word you're saying. Take a deep breath and try again."

She led Darcy to the living room and sat her down on the couch, where she took several deep breaths to try and get her bearings. After a moment, she felt a bit more calm, but she could feel tears streaming down her face she hadn't even realized were there.

"I got into the morgue with no problem. I found the body-- there was only one--and gave him the two drops, just like you told me. I counted off the seconds on my watch while I waited. It only took thirty seconds and then he sat up, he *bolted* up, and his eyes were silver, oh God, they were *silver--*"

Mercy took her by the shoulders again and turned her around so they were eye to eye.

"You aren't making sense, girl, you're babbling! Just calm down," she said in a soft, soothing voice. "You gave him the potion, he woke up. Then what?"

Darcy let out a breath and pushed her hair away from her face. "He was disoriented at first, like you said he would be. But he remembered dying, Mercy. He said he had found his wife on the other side, and when I gave him that potion he was taken from her. He was so angry...I've never heard anything like the sound of his voice."

She began to shiver all over. Mercy tore a colorful afghan off the back of the couch and wrapped it around the girl's shoulders.

"We have to leave, right now," Darcy said. "He knows where you live. We have to go *now*."

"You keep saying that, but where are we going to go?" Mercy said through clenched teeth. "We can't just leave without a plan."

"We'll go to North Carolina," Darcy said quickly. "You were going anyway, so now you'll just go early and take me with you."

Mercy thought about it. She certainly hadn't foreseen such a problem as this; she had assumed that giving someone a second chance at life would leave them indebted to her forever. She had envisioned amassing an army of personal slaves, an army of the undead who would do her bidding. And now this mess.

"Alright," she agreed finally. "Help me pack a few things."

****

That had been the day before, and now Mercy and Darcy sat in the darkened living room of a strange house in Asheville, North Carolina. The previous owners had left some furniture, but most of the pieces were covered in dusty white sheets and Mercy had instructed Darcy not to disturb them. She had spread a blanket on the floor and Darcy had unrolled two sleeping bags, purchased at a Target store one town over. They had stopped there on their way into Asheville, picking up some things to make easy meals as well, and now they munched on cheese and crackers in front of the fire Mercy had built in the fireplace. It had been a damp Spring in Asheville, and the house was chilly and drafty.

"I don't know how long we can stay here," Mercy said, taking a sip of lukewarm tea. She wanted so badly to be in her own home, on her comfortable couch. And really, how much of this was she supposed to take? She had done everything for this brat, and had reaped hardly any benefits!

"I told you, this house has been on the market for almost two years. No one is going to decide to buy it anytime soon. All we have to do is lay low for a little while. Besides, don't you think Karma is at work here? What are the odds that the house closest to Archer's mother would be empty right when we need it? I'm telling you, everything is falling into place."

"I don't know about Karma," Mercy said, stroking her cat, Stormy. They'd had no choice but to bring him along, something Darcy had complained about to no end.

"He *stinks*," she had said when Mercy put his travel cage in the backseat of the car, holding her nose dramatically.

"Well, he hates baths, so it's either deal with the smell or get clawed to death. You wanna try it?"

Darcy had glared at her, and that had been the end of that conversation.

"Tell me again about his mother," Darcy said now, and

Mercy sighed.

"I told you everything already. She's sick. I could almost smell the cancer eating away at her," she said, making a face. "I could tell she wanted me to give her good news, so I lied and said she could have five good years if she took care of herself."

"But you don't think she has that long?" Darcy asked, laying back in her sleeping bag and lacing her hands behind her head.

"Definitely not."

"Well, not that I wish harm on the poor old woman, but if she were to die soon, that could give me an in with Archer," Darcy said.

"Is that all you can think about? My lord, girl, we have more problems than you gettin' close to your movie star. There's a dead man on a rampage back home right now, lookin' for me! I may not be able to go back to my house!"

"I'm sure you knew the risks when you came up with this scheme, didn't you?" Darcy said calmly, without looking at Mercy. "You're a smart woman."

Mercy was rendered speechless for a moment, and Darcy took the opportunity to lay out her plans once more.

"Look, don't worry about going back home. We'll figure something out. Right now we need to focus on one thing at a time. Now, the previous plan involved you getting close with his mother, and I would be introduced as your granddaughter and charm the pants off the old lady, who would then play matchmaker and set me up with her gorgeous single son. Obviously, we can't go that route anymore...but I think you should still keep up appearances. Become friends with her. Take her chicken noodle soup, or something. In the meantime, I need to go to New York and find out what he's doing."

"*What*? I don't think you should travel anymore, Darcy, this is getting to be too dangerous, not to mention expensive--"

"Danger is relative to the plan. I can accept that. And since when are you concerned about money? I have plenty, don't you worry about it."

"Darcy, that money your father left you will only go so

far," Mercy said with a frown. How dare this little brat talk to her like she was a child! "What are you going to do in ten years when it's gone? You've never worked a day in your life. Are you gonna get a job at McDonald's? Be a thirty-year old fry girl?"

"I'm done talking about this. And I don't want to talk about my father. Just know that I am taken care of, and if I want to spend my money on plane tickets to New York, then that's what I'll do."

Mercy set her chin and leaned back against an armchair, staring at the fire.

"I hope you realize the enormity of what I've done for you," she said softly. "And all the while, none of the things I've tried to do have worked out. Maybe I should just focus on my own plans for a while."

Darcy sat up and looked at her, panicked. "No! I mean...please don't. I need you, Mercy. You know I do. And I appreciate everything you've done for me, really. I promise, it won't be too much longer before me and Archer are together. And pretty soon, you'll be able to make all the potions you want. You'll be a millionaire, Mercy! Think of all the people who will want to bring back their loved ones from the dead...and all those who will buy your elixir for themselves, as an extra insurance policy."

"What?" Mercy said. A little bell had gone off in her head. It sounded a lot like a cash register.

"Well, you could sell it to the living as a whatdoyoucallit. You know...provision. Just in case something happens to them, a car accident, say...they'd have your potion on hand to bring themselves back."

Mercy's eyes gleamed in the firelight. "I hadn't thought of that."

"You would be their savior, Mercy," Darcy said softly. "You would have the love and respect of everyone in the country. Maybe even the *planet*."

"I would, wouldn't I?" Mercy asked, and she actually began to get teary eyed at the thought of achieving such success.

Darcy sat back and smiled. It was so easy to make her happy, she thought.

"Listen, why don't you come to New York with me? We'll only be gone a day or two, and then we can come back here and finish working out the plan for going home."

Mercy nodded, still lost in the daydream Darcy had planted in her head.

"You did bring the rest of your stock of invisibility potion, didn't you?" Darcy asked.

"Yes," Mercy said, coming back to reality. She turned to Darcy. "But we have to use it sparingly, because there isn't a lot left. Everything I need to make more is back home."

"That's fine. I don't plan on using it, but I want to know we have some just in case."

And with that, she flipped open her cell phone and began making plans to fly to New York City.

Chapter Eight

"What do you mean, she *lied*?" Archer said through clenched teeth. His hand was wrapped so tightly around his cell phone that his knuckles were white.

"She was afraid she would lose her job," his agent, Steve, said. He had called to tell Archer about the big story, which was all over the gossip columns after it had hit the *Star* that morning. "I know it wasn't the wisest decision on her part, but I don't know if I can blame her. It can't be easy, knowing everyone is going to point the finger at you for a breech in security...for *Archer Black*, no less."

Archer sighed heavily. "I just can't believe she didn't at least come forward to our security people before she went to the press. This is unbelievable."

"Just try to stay calm, Archer. This isn't the end of the world."

"Not the end of the world, no, but when people find out how supposedly easy it is to get to me, they'll all be trying, believe me. I won't have a moment of peace."

"Look, I know how much you value your privacy, but this is just a minor bump in the road. We've got an awesome security team right now and they've been briefed on what's happened. All you need to worry about is resting up for the end of the week, because it's gonna be a bit brutal. You've got four interviews on Thursday alone."

Archer looked at Lucy, who was sitting at the kitchen table with a worried look on her face.

"Fine," he said, relenting. "You're right."

"Look, if you're worried about the press, don't be. Your rep is already strong enough to withstand any sort of gossip column scandal. And it's not like you come off as the bad guy in this; you're the victim, if anything."

"I'm not worried about that. Unless it means a lot of attention in the media, which it probably will."

"You know, for a movie star, you are awfully shy," Steve

said teasingly.

"Yeah, that's what they tell me. I just can't get comfortable with being a celebrity. How does Brad Pitt do it?"

Steve laughed. "Well, he's had a lot of years to get used to it. You will, too, don't worry. It just takes time."

"Thanks. I guess I'll be seeing you in a couple of days."

"Yeah, I'll meet you at your place on Thursday and we'll go to the Hudson Hotel together. That's where I've set up your interviews."

"Sounds good. Thanks again, Steve."

"No problem. Take it easy."

He hung up and looked at Lucy, who was watching him from her spot at the kitchen table and sipping the green tea he'd brought back for her from the coffee shop.

"Everything okay?" she asked softly.

"Yes. It's just that break-in I told you about, in London...the press knows about it now."

"Did they catch the girl who did it?"

"No." He sighed and sat down beside her, gesturing to her cup of tea. He wanted to change the subject. "What does that taste like to you? I mean, does it taste the same as it did before you...you know..."

"Died?"

He nodded, uncomfortable with saying the word out loud. She had assured him she was happy to answer his questions about what things were like for her as a spirit, but he was wary of hurting her feelings.

"I taste it, but it's sort of flat. It's not the tea, it's me. It's like everything is watered down."

"And you don't get hungry or thirsty anymore?"

"No. For a little while after I died, I still wanted food, but I think that was just a reflex. My friend Irish says that things which were important to us in our lives linger after we die. I still breathe, even though I don't need to...it's just habit."

He hadn't noticed before, but she *was* breathing. It was comforting, somehow.

"You've mentioned this Irish person before," he said. "Is he here in the city?" What he didn't say was, *Is he someone I should worry about?*

"Yes. He was the first person I met after I realized I had died. It was comforting, having him there to talk to. I was so alone in that theater, even with a hundred people around me." She smiled and her eyes took on a faraway look, as though she was reliving that day. "He sat down beside me during the movie...it was a Ginger Rogers picture, and he said he was just stopping in to see her, but he sat with me for a moment and told me some important things."

"Like what?" he asked, leaning forward.

"Well, like how to spot another spirit. See, we have these...auras, I suppose you'd call them, over our heads. They can be quite beautiful colors, and they are always bright. They stand out, that's for sure. He told me mine was a--"

"A rainbow," Archer finished for her.

She smiled confusedly. "How did you know that?"

"Because I can see it. Not all the time, but every now and then I catch a glimpse of it. I noticed it last night, right after I woke up."

"Really? How is that possible?"

He shrugged. "I don't know. Maybe because I can see the dead? Although I don't remember ever seeing one around Christina..."

"Are you sure?"

"Not positive, I guess...why? Do you think it means something?"

She frowned. "I don't know. Maybe."

He sensed concern in her voice and smiled. "I'm sure it's fine. It's probably just a side effect of my abilities, which aren't exactly normal to begin with."

She returned his smile, but didn't look convinced. "Maybe."

"Hey, it's okay. I don't like seeing you look so worried."

She smiled and shook her head. "I'm sorry, I know I worry too much. My sisters always gave me grief for it and called me an old lady."

"Well, I may have something that will cheer you up a little, take your mind off things."

He stood up and went to the hall closet, where his jacket was hanging on the doorknob. He rummaged through the pockets for a moment and then came up with a small box wrapped in simple brown paper.

"I saw this in a display window when I went down to get coffee and it made me think of you," he said, placing the box on the table in front of her.

She looked up at him, pleasantly surprised, and smiled. "What is it?"

"Open it and see."

Lucy unwrapped the box gingerly and set the paper aside. The box was unmarked, giving her no clues as to what was inside. She lifted the lid and found, nestled inside several layers of tissue paper, a small water globe. A beautiful ballerina danced beneath the glass dome and when Lucy shook it gently, sparkly snowflakes swirled around, creating a small, beautiful blizzard.

"It's beautiful," she whispered.

"There's a little key on the bottom you can turn to make it play a song," Archer said.

Lucy turned the globe over and found the little silver key. When she wound it, the theme from A Love Story began to play in little tinkly notes.

She listened to the entire song, and when she looked up at him he could see tears sparkling in her eyes.

"What are we doing?" she asked softly.

"What do you mean?"

"I mean, what good can come of this? I see the way you look at me...it's the same way I look at you, Archer," she said boldly. Her cheeks flushed with color and he marveled at how beautiful she was, even as what she was saying began to sink in.

"I think I should leave," she said suddenly, and stood up.

"Wait," Archer said, standing to face her. "Did I do something? Say something? Why do you want to leave now? We don't even know why you're here yet."

"I feel like I'm putting you in danger by being here," she admitted, looking down at her feet. She couldn't bring herself to meet his eyes. "I've had a horrible knot in my stomach all day, like something awful is going to happen. I don't know what it means that you can see my aura, but I don't like it. It doesn't feel right."

"Nothing is going to happen to me," he said, taking her shoulders gently. She looked up at him, her chin tembling as she fought to keep the tears from spilling over, and he brought his hand up to cradle the side of her face. It was like catching a soap bubble in his palm, he marveled; touching her was like touching something delicate that would crumble at the slightest amount of pressure.

"I don't know what I would do if I was responsible for you getting hurt, or....worse," she said. "I can't even think about it without feeling sick to my stomach. And I don't think it matters much at this point that I admit how I feel about you, because I think you already know. I think you started to feel it as soon as you met me." She brought her hand up and placed it over his, leaning into his palm as she did so and closing her eyes. "Didn't you?" she whispered.

He nodded. "Yes."

"We can never be together," she said, and a sob escaped her. "You know that, don't you?"

He leaned forward and pressed his forehead against hers. "Please don't leave me," he said, astounded at the ache that had begun to spread around his heart at the thought of her leaving. "Stay here. Don't give up on me."

She pulled away slightly and looked at him with a mixture of love and exasperation, much as she had Benjamin on the day she died.

"I would never give up on you. I just don't want this to end badly. And I can't see how it could go any other way, Archer. How can this be real? How can I love someone I barely know?"

"I don't pretend to know how it works, and I don't care," he said stubbornly, and he sounded so much like her Benjamin that she laughed through the tears and placed her hands on either side of his face.

"Well, how can I argue with that?" she said, and kissed him.

It was not premeditated, that kiss, merely something that came naturally, and Lucy was just as surprised as Archer when their lips touched. It was quick, not much more than a peck really, but it was the first intimate contact the two of them had shared and it was magical. Time seemed to slow. Both of them had a moment to appreciate the softness of the other's lips, and the strangeness of kissing someone on the opposite side of the line which divided the living and the dead.

Neither was entirely sure who pulled away first, but when Lucy was able to speak again, she looked into Archer's eyes and said, "I guess I'll stay."

****

"Why do you think you are so protective of your privacy?" Lucy asked him later as they sat in front of the fireplace. "You have to admit, acting is a strange profession to take when you don't like to be the center of attention."

"Well, I just sort of fell into acting. It wasn't what I envisioned for myself when I was younger. Actually, I wanted to be an astronaut."

Lucy touched his arm in excitement. "Really? Oh, I am so in love with astronomy! I used to love to lie on my back outside and look up at the stars when I was little. Even as a teenager, I used to picture what space must look like. My father was a great supporter of Albert Einstein, and I remember him telling my sisters and I about how his theory of gravity, how he had proved Sir Isaac Newton wrong by predicting the way the stars moved. It's fascinating, isn't it?"

Archer smiled at her enthusiasm. "Yes, it is. My childhood dream was to train at NASA to be a pilot, but the math always held me back. I'm not very good at it."

"So how did you get into acting?"

He leaned back on his hands and studied the fire. "A friend

127

of my mother's convinced her to enter me into a contest when I was thirteen for "The Next Big Star" on a local television station in my hometown. I didn't win, but an agent saw my head shots and asked to represent me. I guess he saw something the contest judges didn't. I booked my first job two weeks later. It was a commercial for cereal."

Lucy smiled at the thought of a young Archer eating cereal for the cameras.

"And did you love it right away?" she asked.

"I wouldn't say I loved it...but it was extra money, which we needed pretty badly. After my dad died, my mother was left with a bunch of property tax bills for our farm. One night, not long after I got my first acting job, I overheard her crying on the phone. She was telling my aunt that she was afraid we would lose everything because the bills had finally caught up to her. She had taken two jobs after Dad died but it just wasn't enough. So I went to my agent and begged for more auditions. I got three more jobs, and the money from those kept our farm from being foreclosed on."

"Wow," Lucy said softly. "What a wonderful thing to do. Your mother must be so proud of you."

"She is. She's a great lady. I owe so much to her. That's why, when I found out she had cancer last year, I decided to stay in the business rather than quit, like I had been planning. Hospital visits aren't cheap."

Lucy's hand flew to her mouth. "Oh, Archer. I'm so sorry."

"It's okay. She's a strong woman, you know? She's doing okay. Not great, but okay. And if I hadn't continued on this path, I never would have made *Crazy Love*, and you and I never would have met. I would probably be serving coffee in that shop down the street."

"It's just that it must be hard, seeing someone you love suffer from an illness."

"It's the hardest thing I've ever done," he agreed softly. "If she dies, I'll be an orphan. An orphan at the age of 20."

Lucy reached over and took his hand in hers. "I know what that's like."

He looked at her, his face serious. "Yes, I guess you do."

After a moment, she said, "Tell me about your father."

"He was the best man I've ever known," Archer said simply. "He was tireless. He would come home from work some days so exhausted I could see circles under his eyes, but he never complained; he'd just tell me to go get the ball and glove from the barn and we'd play catch until it got too dark outside to see. He loved my mama so much. And she only had eyes for him. It just about killed her when he died."

"How did he die?" she asked gently.

"Heart attack. One day he was there, and the next he wasn't. It was surreal. I don't think it sank in for me until after his funeral. Of course, I dreamed about him right away. And he came to me one night, in my room. Just sat at the foot of my bed and finished the conversation we started in my dream, and then he was gone. I never saw him on the farm again, although Christina and her husband stuck around."

"Did you ever ask them if they had seen your father?"

He shook his head. "I didn't talk about him to anyone but my mama. And Dean...well, I didn't talk to him unless I had no choice. I guess you could say he's the reason I am the way I am."

"What do you mean?"

"He's not a very nice person. He wasn't when he was alive, and I guess it transferred over when he died. He attacked me when I was nine. Left big scratches and bruises all up and down my arms. It sort of scarred me for life. After that I was very protective of my privacy and my personal space."

Lucy's eyes widened. She felt an absurdly strong urge to wrap her arms around him, but kept her distance for the moment.

"And your mother never knew about what was happening?"

"No. I wanted to tell her a million times, but I knew it would scare her. Plus, I was afraid she wouldn't believe me, or worse, that she would think I was crazy and send me away to the loony bin."

"And so, after something that would have made an adult

lose their mind, you just went on with your life and kept your fears to yourself," Lucy observed with awe.

"Kids are resilient," he said. "I bet if the same thing had happened to me for the first time a month ago, I wouldn't have been so cool about it."

"I don't know about that," Lucy said. "You seem like a very strong person to me."

"Well, thanks," he said with a smile. "And thanks for staying."

"Thank you for letting me stay." She drew her knees up to her chest and wrapped her arms around them. "I feel safe here in a way I never did at the theater."

"Good." He reached out and brushed her hair away from her face, making her shiver, and she stood up abruptly.

"I think I'll step out onto the balcony for a moment, if that's okay. I like the way the air smells in the city when Spring is almost over."

He nodded, stifling a yawn. "Okay. I think I might stretch out for just a minute. I haven't been sleeping well..."

He lay back on the rug, folding one arm beneath his head, and closed his eyes.

Lucy opened the French doors that led to the small balcony and looked out over the city, still shaking from the contact she'd had with Archer. Every time he touched her, a jolt went through her body that was almost electric. It was as scary as it was exciting, but she didn't have the strength to tell him to stop.

She looked in at him through the French doors, asleep on the floor in front of the fireplace, and smiled. She couldn't believe she had finally made it here, that she was in the home of the man she had so recently felt an instant attraction to. It seemed almost too good to be true.

And a moment later, when she was no longer standing on the balcony, she wondered if perhaps it was.

****

"Archer?" Lucy called, unable to keep the panic out of her

voice. "*Archer!*"

"I'm here, Lucy," he said, and she turned to find him standing beside a lake.

They were in an unfamiliar place, in the countryside. A low fog crept in over the water, looking for all the world like clouds which had fallen from the gray sky.

She ran to him and he enclosed her in his arms, and the scent and warmth of him was comforting but not enough.

"What's happened? Where are we?" she asked quietly. Something didn't feel right about this place.

"It's okay. You're in my dream," he said calmly. "This is my family's farm."

She pulled away and looked at their surroundings. There was a large weeping willow tree not far from the water which looked vaguely familiar, but she couldn't think of why it should. In the distance was a barn and, beyond that, a house. The fields between them seemed to glow a lush green beneath a fine sheet of dew.

"How did I get here?" she breathed.

"I brought you here," a woman's voice said, and they both turned around.

"Christina," Archer said with a slight frown. "Is everything okay?"

She stepped forward and took Lucy's hand in hers in a welcoming gesture.

"Everything is not okay, I'm afraid," she said to Archer, and then to Lucy, "I'm sorry for pulling you into his dream so abruptly, but I needed to talk to you. Both of you."

"You mean you did this?" Archer said in disbelief.

"Yes," Christina said, looking over her shoulder. "And we don't have a lot of time. You need to listen to me very carefully, alright?"

Archer nodded, his face drawn into a frown of concentration. "Are we in some sort of danger?"

"I think so. There is someone here who can see the other side, like you. She's made friends with your mother. I don't know for sure what she wants yet but I don't trust her, and you shouldn't, either."

"Is she a psychic? My mother said she had met a woman who read tarot cards," Archer said, and Lucy couldn't miss the worry in his voice. She reached out and took his hand.

"Yes. I hid when she came into the house because I sensed something different about her. She has the scent of the dead on her skin."

"What does that mean?" Lucy asked, tightening her grip on Archer's hand.

"It means she draws spirits to her, like our Archer here...but there was something else, something dark. I couldn't quite get a handle on it, but whatever it is, it can't be good. I'm sorry to worry you, especially if it turns out to be nothing. But I'm afraid that if she is getting close to your mother, she could eventually get close to you, Archer...and that could mean trouble."

"You're exactly right. Thank you for warning me," Archer said. He pulled Lucy to him and wrapped his arm around her protectively. "I'm not just looking out for myself anymore."

"So I see," Christina said with a smile. She stepped forward and placed a cool hand on Lucy's cheek, as though searching for fever. After a moment, she pulled away with a satisfied look on her face. "You are a good soul," she said. Her eyes searched Lucy's for a moment, and in them Lucy saw concern for Archer that had been abated, at least temporarily.

"How can you be sure?" Lucy asked, genuinely interested. Christina seemed to take no offense and only shrugged.

"I just can," she said simply. "I've gained a few abilities of my own over the years. I had to, in order to survive here."

She looked around again, as if expecting someone to come along. "You should go. I won't come to you again unless I get more information about this woman."

"Wait!" Archer said, almost angrily. "There are some things I have to know."

"Such as?"

"Such as what that symbol is you had on your hand last time I saw you. Are you controlling my dreams?"

132

She smiled. "I can't control what others do, Archer. If there are spirits who need to come to you in your dreams, I can't stop them--nor would I have reason to. This symbol--" She held up her hand, palm out. "It's an Egyptian hieroglyph. It simply helps you wake up, that's all. I don't want our conversations to be overheard by Dean...I don't want him to know you and I are talking at all. If I sense him coming, this symbol is a way to ensure that you can leave quickly."

Archer seemed satisfied with that answer. "What about the dreams you aren't in? Why can't I remember them? When I wake up, there are only vague images...I can't recall anything that happened. If it is so important for me to listen to what these spirits have to say, why can't I remember?"

"If I had to make an educated guess, I would say it's a defense mechanism. You probably developed it when you were just a child; it's a way to do your job without having to deal with the reprecussions when you wake up. Don't you think it would be damaging to carry around all the pain and grief that is laid upon your shoulders by these spirits? Would you really want to walk around with those thoughts in your head all day?"

"I suppose not, but it's not very reassuring to know my brain is hiding things from me."

"It's probably for the best, Archer. Just remember that."

He sighed and ran a hand through his dark hair. "Alright, I guess that makes sense. But more than that...are you safe here, Christina? Really? Because if you aren't, we should find a way to get you to New York, with me."

She shook her head with a sad smile. "I can't leave here, Archer. I can't explain why just now, but please know that I need to stay. Thank you for your concern, though."

He sighed heavily. "If that's what you want, fine. But if you do decide to leave, you come to me immediately, okay?"

She nodded. "You ready to go back now?"

He looked at Lucy, who nodded her consent. "I suppose so."

Christina began to raise her hand, but Archer stopped her at the last second.

"Wait! I almost forgot..." He paused, looked at Lucy, seemed to gain strength from what he saw in her eyes, and continued. "Have you seen my father here? It's important for me to know that. Have you seen him at all since he died?"

Christina frowned and shook her head slowly. "He won't come back here."

"What? Why not?"

"Because of what Dean told him...he said he would spend the rest of his days trying to hurt you if your father ever set foot on the farm again."

Archer felt his heart speed up, his breath coming faster. "He told my father this...after he died?"

Christina shook her head once more, and now she looked sad. "Oh, Archer, I thought you knew."

"Knew what?" he shouted. "*Tell me!*"

Her eyes brimmed with tears and she wiped them away with the back of her hand.

"Your father could see us when he was alive. He and Dean were...not friendly. Dean wanted you and your family off what he called "his land", and he made sure your father knew it."

He felt breathless, as though someone had just punched him in the gut. "My father...could see spirits?"

"Yes. That's why *you* can see them. He passed on his abilities to his only son like any other gene. I thought you knew."

Archer was shocked speechless. Lucy turned her body into his and brought her hands up gently to his face, forcing him to look at her. She wanted to say something comforting, to tell him it would be alright, but she didn't have a chance. Christina held up her hand, palm out, and flashed the symbol, only it was slightly different this time. There was a circle drawn around the eye in kohl.

"*Remember*," Christina whispered, and the two of them vanished at once.

Mercy, who had already surpassed her tolerance for alcohol that morning, was just tipsy enough to tell her. "I had a spirit come to me several years ago, a young man. He had heard of me from some acquaintance of his and he knew that I could offer the chance to become human again."

"Wait," Darcy interrupted. "Are you talking about the elixir I used on that dead guy? It works on spirits, too?"

"Don't get ahead of yourself, girl," Mercy warned, finishing off her drink. "And keep your voice down. To answer your question, it was a variation on the liquid you used. Anyway, he seemed to genuinely need my help, so I mixed up a batch I had been working on and gave it to him. But as soon as he drank it, I knew it wasn't right. He...he began to convulse. He had a seizure. It was horrible to watch," she said with a shudder.

"My God," Darcy breathed. "Then what happened?"

Mercy's eyes took on a faraway look as she remembered that night. She had suffered nightmares for months afterward, sometimes so bad she chewed on her pillow. One morning she woke up to find a clump of damp feathers in her mouth.

"He changed. Almost before my eyes...it was as though something inside him broke after he took that potion. He turned."

"Like...he was evil?"

"I don't know," Mercy said honestly. "I suppose he was just angry. Like the man you dealt with at the morgue."

"If you knew that was going to happen, why did you send me there?" Darcy hissed angrily. "He could have hurt me, you know."

"Because I *didn't* know that would happen," Mercy said, turning to look at her. "I worked for years on the new elixir, changing the amounts of certain things and adding others. I really thought I got it right this time, I swear I did. I could have sworn I knew what caused the change..."

Darcy had sat back in her seat already, disgusted by the old lady. She had all this power and didn't even know how to use it properly, she thought.

"I thought it was the suicide," Mercy said, and *that* made

Darcy sit up in her seat again.

"What? What did you say about suicide?"

"The man I helped. He had killed himself, you see, and I thought...well, I thought perhaps that was why he became so violent. Something in the chemistry of the brain that changes when you die..."

"And that's why you didn't try it on my mother," Darcy whispered.

"I couldn't watch it happen to her, too," Mercy said sadly. "I just couldn't do it."

"Whatever happened to him? The dead guy?"

"Oh, I took care of him," Mercy said vaguely, shifting again in her seat. "I have a potion for just about everything, dear girl."

Darcy shook her head in disbelief. "Why didn't you tell me about this before now? Do you even realize how dangerous this stuff is? You've been messing with some dark magic, Mercy. I didn't say anything before now because I assumed you knew what you were doing, but I have to say...I don't think you do. I mean, invisibility potion is one thing, but bringing back the dead--"

"*Shut up!*" Mercy hissed. "Just shut up! You don't know what you're talking about! You are a child! I have been doing this since before you were born and I will do it long after you're gone."

With that, she yanked her seat belt off and headed for the restroom, leaving Darcy to stew alone as she tried, unsuccessfully, to push away the thought of her mother coming back from the dead.

****

Mercy slammed the bathroom door behind her and leaned against the sink. Her heart was beating so hard she could see her blouse pulsating slightly with the rhythm.

"Calm down, Mercy," she whispered to herself. "You're alright."

138

But she was not alright. Her left arm felt...tight, as though she was wearing a blood pressure cuff. She had broken out in a cold sweat; it beaded on her forehead and slicked her upper lip.

There was a sudden tap on the door. "Hello?" a woman's voice called.

"Occupied, can't you read?" Mercy snapped. She ran cold water in the sink and splashed some on her face, wishing they would just land already. The airplane was giving her a serious case of claustrophobia; the bathroom alone was the size of a closet. She felt as though she could barely breathe, let alone think, and there was so much to think about...her old friend Alicia, for instance. Oh, how she wished her potion had worked correctly! She could have her best friend here with her now, helping her. Instead she was stuck with Darcy, who, being Alicia's only child, was closest to the real thing.

It was too much. She didn't want to think about it anymore. She looked at herself in the small mirror over the sink and saw an old woman, more gray in her hair than black, and it saddened her. Her chest felt like a weight was sitting on it, and she knew what it meant even if she didn't want to admit it to herself. She stared into her own watery eyes, and after a moment she began to feel a tingle in her fingers and toes. Her hands tightened on the edges of the sink. Her jaw went slack and she began to drool; a long, thin, silvery strand slid down her chin and onto her blouse. Her eyes became unfocused and she fell into the deep, dark pool that always appeared when someone wanted to talk to her.

After a moment, she found herself standing in complete darkness. Suddenly, a small pinpoint of light appeared. It was bright blue in color and slightly diamond shaped; it made her think of starlight in the night sky.

"Mercy, it's me," Alicia said softly.

"Where are you?" Mercy asked, turning a full circle. The space she was in was so dark that she could only see about an inch in front of her face, no more.

"I'm here." A soft hand touched her shoulder and she jumped. But when she turned around, she couldn't see her friend.

"Oh, Alicia," Mercy said with relief. "It's been so long since we talked!"

"I know," Alicia said. "I'm sorry, old friend. I appreciate you taking care of my daughter."

"She misses you so much. I do too," Mercy said with a sniff.

"I know. But we'll be together again someday, won't we?"

"Yes! We will. I've been working on some new things, Alicia, you wouldn't believe how my work has progressed! It's amazing. And Darcy has been such a help to me."

"I'm happy to hear that, Mercy. In fact, I called you here because I have something very important to tell you regarding what you've done so far; you need to give Darcy your notes...everything you have on the potions and your work. Do you understand?"

In the airplane lavatory, Mercy nodded, still with that unfocused expression on her face.

"Yes," Mercy said. "You want me to make sure she knows how to make the potions."

"That's right. Explain to her everything you can remember so that she can pick up where you leave off...in case something should happen to you."

"Am I about to die?" Mercy asked calmly.

"I don't know," Alicia said, although she did. "You can go back now. Darcy will be wondering where you are. But remember: give her all your notes. Don't leave out anything. She needs to continue your work. It could be in our best interest, do you see?"

Mercy smiled and nodded once more. "Of course."

She felt the hand squeeze her shoulder gently and then she was standing in the bathroom again, drooling onto her shirt. Someone was banging on the door.

"I'm coming!" she yelled, grabbing a paper towel to clean herself up. She swiped at her blouse and then wet the paper towel, wiping off her face. A quick look in the mirror showed the same old woman from before; her chest still felt tight and she was white as a sheet, but there wasn't much she could do about that.

"I thought you died in there," the young woman waiting on the other side of the door mumbled as Mercy brushed past her.

"Came close," Mercy said, and something in her eyes made the young woman stumble into the bathroom and slam the door, her heart hammering.

Mercy made her way back to her seat, where Darcy was staring sullenly out the window. When she sat down, she pulled a sheaf of papers from her oversize purse and handed them to Darcy.

"What's this?" Darcy asked, looking suspicious.

"My notes. Not all of them, but the ones that matter. I want you to have them."

"Your notes?" Darcy repeated. "You mean, for the potions?"

"Among other things, yes. The rest of what you'll need is in a locked drawer in my desk. The key is hidden under the velvet lining of my jewelry box."

Darcy glanced at the papers and frowned. The notes were clearly old, as the edges of the pages were yellowed and they had been folded and refolded many times. Mercy's spidery handwriting covered at least thirty pages, perhaps more.

"Why are you giving this to me?"

"I want you to have them in case something happens to me. I want you to continue my work."

"Are you nuts? I don't want to mess with dead people, Mercy. I'm not like you."

Mercy smiled a tight smile and leaned back in her seat. "Your mother suggested that I do this. But if you'd rather not--"

Darcy grabbed Mercy's arm. "You spoke to her? Just now? What did she say?"

"I just told you what she said. She wants you to learn what I do, Darcy. You could be the one who sets her free someday."

Darcy stared at Mercy in shock, her mouth hanging open. She didn't know what to say. She had never imagined that Mercy would hand down the potion recipes to her, and she had certainly never entertained the idea of working with the dead...

"How would this work?" she asked softly. "I can't speak to spirits like you can."

"Haven't you ever heard of a person being haunted?" Mercy said with a strange little smile. "The spirits will come to you. You just have to open yourself up to it."

And with that, they began their descent into New York City.

Chapter Ten

When Archer awoke, his head was thumping like a bass drum. He sat up, wincing at the pain in his lower back, and realized Lucy was still asleep at his side. They were both on the hard floor of his apartment. The light outside the windows was cold and gray, and it was too dark to still be morning. He glanced at the clock on his nightstand and was astonished to find that they had slept through the night and most of the afternoon. It was four o'clock.

He put his head in his hands and rubbed his eyes, surprised he could remember the entirety of his dream; he wondered if Christina had something to do with that. Come to think of it, he usually remembered more when she was present. He'd never realized it before, but wondered now what it meant.

He heard a whimper at his side and turned to find Lucy awake, her eyes brimming with tears. She looked up at him sadly and sat up, wrapping her arms around her knees.

"I'm sorry, Archer. About your father."

"Thank you. It probably shouldn't come as such a surprise to me. Dean dropped a hint earlier that he's spoken to my father before; I should have realized the truth then. I guess I was just preoccupied."

He smiled weakly to show Lucy that he was okay, but she moved suddenly against his chest, laying her ear over his heart and wrapping her arms around his waist. He brought his hands up to stroke her hair gently, amazed as ever at the feel of her. He wondered what he felt like beneath her hands and said so aloud.

"Strange," she answered without looking up at him. "Like I might fall right through you when we hug."

She pulled away and stood up, crossing her arms in front of her and cupping her elbows in her hands. It was a gesture that reminded him terribly of his mother and his heart ached at the thought.

"That's why I've decided I need to leave," Lucy said

143

suddenly. She had gone to the window to look out at the street below and her back was to him, but he could tell by the way her shoulders were hunched that she was crying even harder than before.

"What? Why?"

"I told you before, Archer. The things I feel about you...it's too much. I've never felt this way about anyone. But every time I touch you, it's a reminder of how different we really are."

He stood and went to her, placing a gentle hand on her arm. "Why are you so scared?" he asked.

She flung his hand off angrily and spun around. "I am *not* scared! You don't know what it's been like for me all these years, going through existence with no one around me that I care about, having to watch my family members die and then having my heart broken when they don't show up on this side! I ask myself *every day* why I was chosen to come back as a spirit alone, and do you know what? I don't have an answer."

Archer placed his palm on the window, letting the coldness of the day seep under his skin. "I'm sorry. I know it must be hard for you."

"It is!" she cried, and the tears began to flow harder. She wiped them away with the back of her hand and shook her head. "I was so excited when I found you and realized that you could see me, hear me, touch me! You'll never know what it's meant to me, Archer." She paused and closed her eyes. "I've been alone for so long," she moaned.

"Then why do you want to leave?" he asked. The lump in his throat was making it hard to speak.

"Because we can never be together," she said sadly. "I can't spend the rest of my days loving someone who can't love me back."

"But I do love you. I've never known anyone like you, Lucy. I've never...I haven't met anyone I felt I could love until you came along," he said, the softness in his voice betraying the way he felt. He wanted to scream, take her by the shoulders and make her listen. But he knew it would do no good.

"Stop," she said, smiling a wounded smile. It was an odd

juxtaposition, that smile with the tears still streaming down her cheeks. "I've gotten in way over my head here, Archer. And every day I spend with you is a day that I get deeper and deeper. I feel like I was meant to meet you but I don't know why, and I feel like I should be helping you with something but I don't know what. There's an odd feeling in my gut sometimes, like I'm missing something important. It's a bad feeling, like there's danger ahead. I feel like...like I might be putting you in danger by being here."

"Please don't go," he said, clenching his jaw. He couldn't find the right words anymore; his tongue felt glued to the roof of his mouth. His heart hammered in his chest and he felt a cold sweat break out on his forehead, but still he didn't know what to do, what to say, to make her stay. He leaned down and pressed his forehead against hers. "I don't know what else to say, just please don't go."

She placed a hand on his cheek and he turned his face into her palm, closing his eyes against what he knew was coming.

"I have to," she said simply, and when he opened his eyes she was gone.

****

Darcy and Mercy arrived in New York and went straight to their hotel, a small, out-of-the-way place Mercy had never heard of. It was sandwiched between an office building and a restaurant specializing in Indian food, and the entire block smelled like curry. But the inside of the hotel was nice enough, she supposed, so she didn't complain. She knew Darcy had wanted to keep a low profile while in town, although she had been pleasantly surprised by the headline plastered on the front page of several newspapers at the newsstand outside the hotel: *"Archer Black has uninvited guest in London hotel!"*

"Check it out, Mercy, I'm famous!" Darcy had crowed, picking up a paper to scan the article.

"Keep your voice down, unless you want to be the most popular girl in the New York City Jail," Mercy said.

Darcy had waved a hand dismissively at her, ready to stand on the street and read the entire article before Mercy had reminded her of more important things; namely, bumping into Archer.

"Besides, I need to get my baby upstairs and feed him," Mercy said, gesturing to the pet crate she was carrying laborously. Stormy meowed pitifully inside, his green eyes almost glowing from the depths of the carrier.

"Ugh, why did you have to bring him, anyway? We could have left some food out for him back at the house. We'll only be here for a day."

"Because he needs his medicine," Mercy said. "He has to have it every day."

"Fine," Darcy said, tossing the newspaper back on top of the stack. "Ruin my moment, why don't you?"

"You really need to be careful about what you say around here," Mercy reminded her once they were in the elevator on the way to their room. It was a rickety old thing and there was no attendant, but at least they were alone. "I know it's a big city, but when it comes to celebrities it can be smaller than you think. If anyone even gets a whiff of what we're doing and the things we've done, it will be over for us, do you understand?"

"Yes, yes, I get it, you don't have to keep drilling it into my head. I'm not an idiot."

"Being an idiot has nothing to do with it, Darcy. Even the smartest people make mistakes."

Darcy didn't reply, just kept her eyes on the numbered buttons on the elevator wall, watching as they lit up for each floor they passed. Finally, they reached the twelfth floor and the door slid open with a *thump*.

"Nothin' to write home about, I know, but it'll work for tonight," Darcy said once they were inside their room. She took the potion out of her bag and sat it carefully on the television stand, not wanting to leave it unprotected in her purse any longer than she had to. Then she flung her bag onto the bed and went straight to the window, pushing it open after a moment of struggle. A slight breeze was carried in, redolent of curry and car exhaust.

"Lovely," Mercy said under her breath. She sat Stormy's cage on the bed and opened it, allowing him to walk slowly out, stretching his legs as he did so. She dug a small bottle out of her purse and unscrewed the cap, pulling out a dropper with orange liquid inside.

"What is that stuff, anyway?" Darcy asked, watching Mercy as she let Stormy lick the medicine from the tip of the dropper.

"It's an antibiotic," she replied, making sure the cat took every drop of the liquid. "He was in a fight with another cat not long ago and his little ears got scratched up."

This was a lie, of course, but Mercy didn't want Darcy to know the truth yet. This was something just for her, something close to her heart, and she didn't have to tell anyone if she didn't want to.

"I've never seen an animal take medicine so well," Darcy remarked.

"He's a good boy, aren't you, Stormy? He loves his mommy."

"Yeah," Darcy said, rolling her eyes at Mercy's patheticness. "Well I'm gonna freshen up and then head downtown. I shouldn't be gone long. What are you going to do tonight?"

"Probably just watch some television," Mercy said, putting away the medicine bottle. "Mind if I get into the bathroom first so I can fill up Stormy's water dish?"

Darcy gestured for the older woman to go ahead and sat on the bed to wait. Stormy nudged the back of her hand with his head, clearly wanting his ears scratched, and she obliged without even thinking about it. Her mind was on other things...like that orange medicine. It seemed odd to her that Mercy would give the cat oral medicine for a scratch on his ear. Not only that, hadn't Mercy's eyes darted to the left when she talked about it? As though she wasn't quite telling the truth...

Keeping her eyes on the bathroom, she leaned over and nudged Mercy's purse so the medicine bottle was visible. It didn't look like any antibiotic she'd ever seen; it didn't even have a label. It was in a small vial similar to the ones she kept the invisibility potion in. Strange.

"Okay, I'm all finished. You'd better hurry if you want to catch him at the coffee shop, it'll be dinner time soon," Mercy said, coming out of the bathroom with the cat's water.

"Yeah, thanks," Darcy said, pushing the cat away from her. And in her excitement at the prospect of seeing Archer again, the medicine bottle was thrown from her mind. She danced into the bathroom to get ready.

****

Fate. It's existence is something argued about by many, but proven by none. It is something which some of us want desperately to believe in, because it means that everything is out of our hands; we are responsible for nothing. And when the wind blows someone or something our way, we know that it was predestined. There was nothing that could have been done to change or stop it.

But for others, this is the very reason the idea of fate is so scary. For these people, the knowledge that everything that happens in life--and after--is controlled by an unseen force is too terrifying to think about.

Darcy belongs to the former school of thought; Lucy, the latter; and Archer, an odd mixture of the two.

He was born into a family of church goers, good Christian people who believed that the answer to life's questions could be found in faith. In a way, it was comforting to believe that things were out of his hands, that some greater power was watching over him and blocking 89% of any harm that could come his way. But when his father died, he began to question this faith. He wondered if perhaps it was more harmful to trust in something he couldn't see than to take responsibility for things; and that is why he feels such guilt over the death of his father. It is why he feels the need to protect Lucy and Christina, more so than out of some gentlemanly need to display his Southern manners.

If he had known what the next several hours were going to bring to him, he would have begun to rethink his stance on fate. He would have been more observant of his surroundings. He would have noticed the pale face peering in at him through the French doors leading to the balcony as he spoke to Lucy, and he might not have been surprised to see, when he confronted the owner of that face, a small pink tattoo on her wrist.

Not much surprised him anymore, you see.

****

"I don't care if you're in your nightgown, throw on a long coat and get over here now," Darcy hissed into her cell phone. She was standing in the shadows behind Archer's apartment building, her cheeks burning from a mixture of anger and humiliation.

"Darcy, what is this all abou--" Mercy began, but Darcy cut her off.

"It's about you giving someone else that invisibility potion," Darcy said, and her voice was deadly.

"What are you talking about? No one knows about that but you, I swear!"

"Then tell me why I just saw Archer in his apartment, talking to someone who isn't there?" Darcy asked, looking around her to make sure no one was listening.

"What are you doing at his apartment? I thought you were going to meet him at a coffee shop?"

"Well, that was the plan, but he never showed up. I know for a fact that he goes there at least once a day, he's made the place famous. So when he didn't come I asked the guy behind the counter if he had seen him today, and he said he hadn't. I got worried. So I used my powers of persuasion to get the guy to tell me where Archer lives. I snuck up onto his balcony-- luckily the apartment next to his is empty, so I just jimmied the lock and came in through there so I could crawl over to his patio--and looked in, and what did I see? Archer Black, sitting

149

on the floor and talking to someone I can't see!"

"Are you *mad*?" Mercy asked. She knew Darcy had it bad for this guy, but this was ridiculous! "You don't even have the invisibility potion with you, and I know that because it's sitting here on the t.v. stand! You're telling me you risked being seen so you could crawl onto his balcony and stalk him?"

"*I am not stalking him!*" Darcy shrieked. She didn't care anymore if someone heard her. "I was worried about him! And now apparently the one person I thought I could trust has betrayed me. Who did you sell it to, Mercy? And don't lie to me."

"Darcy, I swear to you, I didn't sell anyone anything. Are you sure there wasn't someone in another room? Maybe just out of sight?"

"It wasn't like that," Darcy said, shuddering as she recalled seeing him wrap his arms around what appeared to be thin air. "Someone was sitting next to him. If it wasn't an invisible person, then I want to know what is going on."

Mercy sighed heavily. "Alright, I'll come down there. Give me ten minutes."

"Make it five. And bring the potion with you," Darcy said, and hung up.

Chapter Eleven

"Mercy? Where are you?"

Darcy stood in the deep shadows beside Archer's apartment building, holding her hands out in front of her like a blind person. She had never been on the other side of the invisibility potion before, and it was no fun. She felt like Mercy was going to sneak up behind her and scare the bejesus out of her.

"I'm here, child," Mercy said from her left. Darcy turned in that direction and pointed to the balcony that she knew belonged to Archer.

"He's on the tenth floor," she said. "The one with the green curtains. I didn't lock the door behind me when I left the apartment next door, so you can go through there to get out on the balcony."

"You must be insane," Mercy hissed. "I didn't even want to take this potion in the first place, you know it's hard on me! There is no way I'm climbing onto balconies!"

Darcy sighed. "Fine. How are you going to see what's going on, then?"

"I'll figure something out," Mercy said huffily. "Wait here."

Darcy felt a slight breeze brush past her arm as Mercy walked by. After a moment, she crept to the corner of the building and peeked around to the front door, where a man was using his key to get in. She watched him step inside and, a moment later, the door swung back on its hinges as though someone had caught it before it closed completely.

"Hmph," Darcy muttered. "Nice work, Mercy."

****

Someone rapped on Archer's door three times, quickly and efficiently. He jumped up from the bed, where he had been sitting with his head in his hands, and ran to answer it.

"Lucy?" Archer said as he flung open the door. But there was no one there. He stepped out and looked up and down the

151

hallway, confused as to how anyone could have left so quickly. But the corridor was empty, so he stepped back into his apartment and closed the door. He never felt the slight breeze brush by his arm; he was too preoccupied with his thoughts.

Lucy was gone. He had no idea if she would come back, even if he went to the Imperial and begged her to. She had made up her mind, it seemed.

He lay on his bed and covered his eyes with his arm. He could smell her on his pillowcase, a scent like oranges and honeysuckle that always lingered in her hair, and his stomach tightened. Had he really just lost the only girl he had ever had feelings for?

The ringing of his cell phone jarred him back to the present and he grabbed it off his nightstand, not bothering to look on the caller ID to see who it was.

"Archer? It's June."

He sat up in bed, heart thudding. After Lucy had left, he'd forgotten all about their shared dream--and about Christina's warning. He had planned to call his mama as soon as he woke up but there hadn't been time. And now something had happened; he could feel it.

"June? What's wrong?"

She didn't reply right away, but she didn't have to. Her sniffles told him everything he needed to know. He leaned his head back against the headboard and squeezed his eyes shut, willing the hot lump in his throat to go away so he could speak. When it didn't, he let the tears come freely.

"I'm so sorry, honey," June said softly. "She went in her sleep."

****

By the time Mercy came back downstairs, she was showing signs of becoming visible again. Darcy watched the front door open--seemingly by itself--and then heard footsteps treading on the sidewalk towards her. As Mercy walked under the streetlights, Darcy could see shimmers of pink and gold from her shirt, and her hair was already mostly visible. It was certainly a creepy sight, even to Darcy, who knew how it worked.

"So? What happened? Did you see anything? Where did you go?"

Mercy brushed past her and walked around the corner of the building, where she could wrap herself in shadows to keep from being seen. Darcy followed her eagerly.

"I knocked on his door, and when he answered it I just sort of slipped in," Mercy said with a smug smile. In the shadows, it reminded Darcy of the Cheshire cat's grin. "I stood in the corner and waited for something to happen, but he was alone."

"What? Are you sure?"

"I'm positive. But I think you're right about someone being there before...it was a girl named Lucy. He was thinking about her the entire time I was up there, thoughts so strong I picked up on them right away. Usually I have to have my crystals or initiate skin-to-skin contact with a person to read their thoughts."

Darcy frowned. "I didn't know you could do that. Have you ever read mine?"

Mercy inclined her head. "I don't make a habit of peeking on other people's thoughts when I get the notion. That would be unethical and besides, I don't know if I *want* to know what some people are thinking." She shuddered at the very idea. "But there are times, when someone has a very strong energy, that I am able to pick up on feelings and memories. They mostly come as images in my head, but sometimes I hear voices, too."

"Why do you think you were able to read his mind so easily?"

"Well, I'm not sure...but I think it's because he and this Lucy girl have such a strong bond. It was amazing, the intensity I got from him. He practically could have lit his apartment with the energy he gave off."

"A strong bond. Great. I traveled all the way here for a guy and he's already got a girlfriend!" She leaned against the brick wall of the apartment building and slumped down until she was sitting on the cold concrete of the alleyway. "When did this happen? And who is she, anyway? The Invisible Woman?"

"Not invisible," Mercy said, shaking her head. "A spirit."

Darcy narrowed her eyes at Mercy. "What?"

"Your Archer is in love with a ghost. But I wouldn't worry too much about her. She just left him, apparently. And that's not all," she went on as Darcy reeled. "His poor sick mama just died."

Darcy shot up from the ground and grabbed Mercy by the shoulders. "Are you kidding me?"

Mercy shook her head. "Not one bit."

"My God," Darcy said, pushing her hair out of her eyes and pacing back and forth. Her eyes focused on nothing in particular as the wheels turned in her head, already planning their next move. "Do you know what this means?"

Mercy sighed. "I hope it means we can go home now. I'm so *tired*."

"Soon, Mercy. But first I need to know something."

"What's that?"

Darcy smiled sweetly. "Do you know where we might find this Lucy girl?"

Mercy thought about it for a moment. "Archer kept thinking about something called Imperial something-or-other. Does that mean anything to you?"

And Darcy, who was indeed familiar with the Imperial Theater, nodded her head.

****

Lucy sat in her usual seat at the Imperial after closing, willing her thoughts to leave her alone. But her mind and heart worked together most of the time, and all she could see when she closed her eyes was Archer's face; all she could think of was the pleading note in his voice when he had begged her not to go. Was she being selfish again, the same way she had been with Benjamin? She thought perhaps she was, and the guilt came crashing down on her. If she had told Ben she loved him before she died, would it have made a difference to him when he decided to kill himself? Maybe a few well chosen words could have saved him, even if they were not completely true.

Her body physically ached in rhythm with her heart at the thought of something happening to Archer. *How is it possible to feel this much pain when you aren't even alive?* she wondered.

"This is the second time I've come across you in here with tears in your eyes, Miss Lucy," Irish said from behind her, and she jumped and spun around in her seat. "If I didn't know any better I'd say you had a broken heart."

She swiped at her eyes and was mildly surprised to find that he was right; she had been crying. She hadn't even noticed.

"I do, Irish. And it's all my fault. I am a selfish, horrible person."

"Now, now, I won't let you talk about my friend that way," he said, sitting down beside her. "She's one of the best people I know." He pulled a handkerchief out of his pocket and handed it to her. It was rumpled but clean.

"I appreciate that you think so, Irish, but sometimes I wonder. Sometimes I feel like the most rotten person who ever lived. And died."

"I can tell. Your aura is looking mighty low, you know."

She turned to him, all thoughts of Archer swept away for the moment in her curiosity. "My aura? What do you mean?"

"Well, an aura is very closely connected to the way we feel at any given time. It's sort of an indicator of our...energy, I suppose. And darlin', right now yours is as dim as dirty dishwater. Shame, really, because normally it's a beautiful thing to behold."

She thought about that for a moment. "Irish, can I ask you something? You seem to know a lot about these things."

"'Course you can."

"What do you think it would mean if a living person could see my aura?"

He smiled and propped his legs up on the seat in front of

him, displaying a pair of old and very worn boots. "Oh, I don't think you have to worry about that, Miss Lucy. The chances of that happening are slim to none."

"But what if it *did* happen? Is it bad?"

His handsome face turned serious as he nodded. "Pretty bad, Miss. A living person who could see an aura...well, that person would be in great danger. In fact, that person would be knocking on death's door."

"*What*?" Lucy cried, sitting straight up in her seat.

"It's alright, Miss Lucy," Irish said, alarmed. He put a hand on her arm to calm her, but she was staring at him in horror. "It's so rare that you'll never have to--"

"Do you mean to tell me that a person who can see my aura is about to die?" she asked. Her voice shook.

Irish nodded slowly. "I'm afraid so, darlin'. Only someone who was close to coming over to the other side would be able to pick up on your energy."

Lucy jumped up from her seat and ran down the aisle, picking up her skirt as she did so to keep from tripping over the hem.

"I'm sorry, I have to go," she called over her shoulder. "Thanks, Irish!"

She hurried out into the main lobby of the theater and willed herself through the outer doors. In a moment she was outside, breathing in the crisp air. She turned in the direction of Archer's place and was just wondering if she should hitch a ride with a cab when she noticed an older lady walking quickly towards her on the sidewalk. The woman was staring right at her.

"Lucy?" the woman asked as she came to a stop in front of her. "Is that your name?"

Lucy peered intently at the woman, trying to remember if she had ever met her, and found she couldn't. But the woman didn't have an aura, which meant she was one of the living. *And she could see Lucy.*

"I'm Lucy," she said softly, crossing her arms in front of her as though she were cold. "May I ask who you are?"

"My name is Mercy," the older woman said. She had a deep southern accent and was wringing her hands as though she was upset over something. "I'm a good friend of Archer Black's family."

"Archer?" Lucy suddenly felt dizzy and heard her own voice in an echo, as though from far away; this was it, then. This woman, who could somehow see the dead as Archer could, had come to give her the news. *He's killed himself, she thought*. And it is all my fault. "Is everything okay?"

"I'm afraid not, honey. His mama has died. He's going home tonight...right now, as a matter of fact. He asked me to come tell you because I'm a seer, like he is. He knew I would find you."

"Oh," Lucy said, putting a hand to her stomach. She felt like she was going to be sick, a feeling she hadn't had in many years. Relief flooded through her and made her knees weak, and Mercy reached out and steadied her with a firm hand.

"Are you alright?" Mercy asked.

"Yes. I need to be with him, can you take me?" Lucy asked breathlessly. She couldn't help but be relieved that he was okay, but she knew he would be devastated about the loss of his mother, whom he obviously adored.

"Of course, child. Come with me," Mercy said with a comforting smile, and wrapped her arm around Lucy's shoulders. To the passerby on the streets, she looked like any number of senile old ladies who talked to no one in particular.

And Lucy, who was so relived that Archer was unharmed and alive, didn't recall the dream she had shared with him, or the words of warning that Christina had given about a strange psychic woman who had ties to the dead.

Chapter Twelve

Archer had come very close to going to the Imperial so he could track down Lucy before he left for home, but as he threw a few changes of clothes into a bag he had second thoughts.

His mind was a jumbled mess, full of images of home and the memory of the way his mama's voice had sounded the last time they had spoken; she had been so happy, jubilant almost. And she had been so sure that everything was looking up as far as her health went...but it had all been for nothing. He wondered if she had even been pretending she felt better for his sake. Perhaps she knew that her time was short and hadn't wanted him to worry.

She was gone. He couldn't imagine ever smiling again, not with both she and Lucy out of his life. To make matters worse, he hadn't even been able to ask her the questions he had about his father, such as whether she had known about his abilities before he died. He felt he would never know. Because, even though he shared his father's gift for seeing and speaking to the dead, he felt instinctively that his mother wouldn't come to him; she wouldn't want to be a burden or cause him any heartache, just as his father hadn't. He had a feeling they both felt that staying away was easier on everyone than hanging around, dredging up old hurt.

He felt as though his world had been turned upside down. And he was all alone.

And even though he was a complete mess and his thoughts were unglued to say the least, he did remember the warning that Christina had given him about the psychic woman who had befriended his mother. As much as he wanted to find Lucy and ask her to accompany him to North Carolina, his fear for her safety took precedence. He would never put her in danger, even if she didn't feel they could be together.

He picked up the phone and dialed his agent to let him know what was going on.

Lucy awoke slowly and lifted her head with effort. Her eyes were blurry and for a moment she felt real panic, something she hadn't felt in a long time. But after a moment, her vision began to clear and she was able to see the room she was in. It was dim, with a thin sliver of light streaming in through the one window that was placed high up on the wall. It appeared she was in a basement room of sorts, but it didn't look familiar, and she couldn't recall how she had gotten here.

She couldn't move her arms.

Her fingers tingled strangely and she looked down at her hands, which were folded in her lap. She sat in a wooden chair and she wasn't bound in any way, yet she couldn't lift her arms or move her legs at all, and her extremities felt as though they had gone to sleep--something else she hadn't felt in a long while.

Hushed voices floated under the closed door and she tried to turn her head to see if someone was coming in, but even that was impossible.

"I told you, I took care of it," a familiar voice was saying.

Suddenly, the door was pushed open and two women came in. The younger one, a pretty girl with long dark hair, was a stranger, but the older one was the lady who had come to tell Lucy about Archer.

Oh, Archer! she thought. *Poor Archer.* His mother had died...she remembered now. He would be so upset, and she wasn't even with him to give comfort.

"Well, well, she's awake," the young one said. She had folded her arms across her chest defensively and was glaring at Lucy with open animosity.

"I told you it didn't last too long," the older woman said. *Mercy*, Lucy thought. *She said her name was Mercy.*

"What's wrong with me?" Lucy asked. Her voice was slurred, as though she had just drank a pint of whiskey. The left side of her face felt frozen, making it even harder to speak. "Why can't I move? Where am I?"

159

"You sure ask a lot of questions for someone who's here to answer them," the dark-haired girl said.

"I...I don't understand what you mean..." Lucy said. It was taking so much effort to speak, and she was so *tired.* "I thought you were bringing me to see Archer."

"Oh, he'll be here," the girl said with a smirk. The older woman, Mercy, was standing in the corner with her hand over her heart. She didn't look well, Lucy thought. Her face was an ashen color and she had bluish circles beneath her eyes. A fine sheen of sweat glistened on her upper lip.

"Darcy, I need to go sit down," Mercy said, leaning against the wall for support. "I'm really not feeling so hot."

Darcy ignored her and kept her eyes on Lucy. "How do you know Archer?"

Lucy tipped her head back; it felt so heavy, much too heavy to be supported by her neck. She wanted to close her eyes and sleep...perhaps if she could take a nap, she would dream about Archer. She could tell him how sorry she was about everything, and then--

WHAP!

A cool hand smacked her across the face, hard enough to rock her head back even further. She cried out and tried to bring her hands up to block any oncoming blows, but her arms were still immobile.

"Answer me!" Darcy yelled. She leaned over until she was mere inches from Lucy's face. "How do you know him?"

Lucy felt hot tears of shame and fear streak down her cheeks and kept her eyes averted from Darcy's, afraid that eye contact would only bring more violence.

"I haven't known him long, I saw him in a movie and came to New York to meet him," she whispered.

"You...saw him in a movie?" Darcy asked incredulously. And then she began to laugh. It was a horrible sound to Lucy's ears, because it was the sound of madness and anger and envy all rolled into one. "All this trouble because a dead girl saw Archer Black in a movie and developed a crush!"

She leaned against the wall behind Lucy's chair and

160

laughed hysterically, sliding down the cement blocks after a moment and collapsing into a fit of giggles.

Lucy's head was laying against her shoulder, which made her point of view slightly off; the entire room was tilted at an angle. She felt her stomach do a slow roll and used all her strength to try and move her head so that she could see things properly.

"She's getting stronger," Mercy said from the corner, where she was still leaning with her hand on her chest. "It's almost time."

"Time for what?" Lucy asked. With her words slurred, the sentence came out *Ti' fa wha'?*

Darcy stopped laughing abruptly and stood up, coming to Lucy's side and pushing her hair out of her eyes. "Time for our favorite movie star to come running in and save you."

Lucy felt her eyes, the only part of her body she could actively control, widen to roughly the size of dinner plates. She remembered--too late, much too late--Christina's warning about the strange psychic woman who had befriended Archer's mother...the same woman who could communicate with the dead, just like Mercy. And now that Darcy was standing so close to her, she could see the small pink tattoo on her wrist: the initials A.B.

"I know who you are," Lucy whispered, forcing her tongue to make the syllables strong and clear with effort.

Darcy smiled and caressed Lucy's cheek almost lovingly. After a moment, her hand slid up into Lucy's hair and twisted it, wrapping the strands around her fist. Lucy cried out weakly as her head was jerked back and Darcy leaned down so that they were eye to eye.

"You may know my name, girl, but you will *never* know me. And you will never know what I am capable of."

"Archer will never love you," Lucy said boldly. Her voice was soft but the power of her words forced Darcy to let her go and take a step back. For a moment Lucy could almost see the hatred shimmering in the air between them, and then Darcy smiled once more.

"Oh, Lucy," she said, shaking her head as though she felt sorry for her. "There are a lot of things you know nothing about. That's just one more."

She turned and motioned to Mercy, who followed her from the room.

And suddenly, Lucy remembered what Irish had told her at the Imperial; the fact that Archer could see her aura meant he was in grave danger. And here she was, unable to get to him, unable to even move.

Oh, Archer, where are you? Lucy thought miserably.

****

Archer was sitting in a cab, slowly winding his way through the rain-slogged roads of Asheville. He had come alone, although Steve had offered to make the trip with him.

"You shouldn't be by yourself right now, Archer," Steve had said with his voice full of concern. "I can call someone for you if you need me to. Do you have any family you'd like to notify?"

"Thanks, but I can do that. Don't worry, I'll be fine," Archer said. "Do you think it will be a problem to cancel my schedule for a couple of weeks?"

"No worries. Let me handle all that. You just get home and spend some time with your family. And Archer, I'm so sorry."

"I appreciate that. I'll call you sometime this week and let you know when I can make it back to the city."

But he wondered later, as he sat in the backseat of a cab older than he was, if he would make that call at all. Knowing his mother was gone was enough to make him rethink his career. He entertained thoughts of moving back home, tending the farm, spending his days by the lake and his nights on the wraparound porch, where he could watch the sun go down behind the pines. There were no nights like that in New York; you could barely see the stars above the rooftops. He wanted to feel a breeze on his face that didn't stink of car exhaust.

"You need help with your bags, sir?" the cabbie asked,

breaking into his thoughts.

"No thanks," Archer replied, looking out his window. His childhood home was coming up on the left, looking the same as it always had, much to his relief. He had expected it to be changed, much the same as his own life now was. "I don't have much with me."

The driver brought the cab to a stop beside the mailbox and Archer stepped out, stretching his legs for a moment before grabbing his bag from the back seat. He handed the cabbie a twenty dollar bill and told him to keep the change, eliciting a surprised "Thanks" from the older man. He drove slowly away, leaving Archer alone with an empty house.

On impulse, he checked the mailbox before heading down the steep driveway and found a single envelope inside. His mouth suddenly went dry and his palms were slicked with sweat as he recognized the glittery pink ink in which his name was written.

He dropped his bag to the muddy surface of the road and tore the envelope open with shaking hands. Inside was a single sheet of paper, containing a short note written in that same glittery ink.

Archer,

I know how sad this day is for you, but please believe me when I tell you that it could get much worse if you do not do as I say. Take your things into your house and meet me at the old Stevenson house up the road. Come alone. I will be waiting for you, darlin'.

--Darcy

Archer immediately looked around him to see if he was being watched, but the road was empty on both sides. The Stevenson house was up around the bend, too far away for him to see from where he stood. He briefly entertained the idea of looking for one of his dad's old guns in the house, but the sudden knot that had formed in his stomach told him there wasn't time for that. He thought of Lucy and wondered if any of this involved her. He felt his hands clench into fists at the idea.

If someone had hurt Lucy, they would pay.

****

Darcy stood at the living room window with her arms crossed, watching for any sign of Archer. Stormy wound through her legs, purring indignantly as she ignored him.

"I think I should lie down," Mercy said. She had been sitting in an armchair beside the fire for over an hour now, complaining of not feeling well. Darcy rolled her eyes without turning around and flapped a dismissive hand at her.

"Go ahead. Just don't fall asleep, I may need you later."

Mercy hauled her bulk off the chair and walked slowly up the stairs to find a bed, clicking her fingers for Stormy to follow her. But the cat stayed where he was, watching Darcy intently as if to see what she would do next.

"There he is," she said softly, smiling when she saw that Archer was alone as she had demanded. He walked slowly up the middle of the road, eying the house warily. She stood back, away from the window, and waited for him to knock on the door.

****

Lucy found that as the minutes ticked by, she could gradually move more and more. She wiggled her fingers, which still tingled but were more mobile than before. Her arms felt incredibly heavy but after a few tries, she discovered she could lift them a few inches into the air.

What had they given her? She felt more than drugged; it was as though she had fallen asleep and then woken up in a different body. But it was her own, she was sure of that. Her hands *looked* the same, even if they felt foreign. More worrisome was the unknown; would there be aftereffects? Would she ever gain complete use of her limbs again? And what could Mercy and Darcy possibly have access to that would affect a spirit in such a way?

Suddenly, she heard loud voices from upstairs. She recognized Darcy's, but there was now a man up there...

Archer! She would know his deep voice anywhere. He must have figured out where she was and had come to rescue her! But he was in danger and had no idea...

"Archer!" she called. In her head, it was a scream. But in reality, it was barely more than a whisper. Her vocal chords felt tight, like they hadn't been used in a while.

"Is she here?" she heard him ask, and it sounded as though he was tantalizingly close to her. *He must be standing directly over my head*, she thought.

"Who are you referring to?" Darcy asked sweetly.

There was a sudden loud thump and a cry of pain; the floorboards creaked and drifted dust down into Lucy's lap. She looked up and found she could see their shadows moving up there through the thin gaps in the hardwood.

"Don't play games with me!" Archer shouted. "I know it was you in my hotel room in London. What I don't know is why you made me come here. And I'm telling you right now, if you've done something to Lucy, I will lose what little restraint I have left."

"I brought you here so we could be together," Darcy simpered. "I know you probably think it was awfully forward of me to come see you in London, but I just wanted to let you know how much your number one fan loves you."

Lucy lifted her arm again and got it higher this time than ever before. She spoke Archer's name once more, a little louder.

Time was getting short.

****

"You think I want to be with you?" Archer asked, disgusted.

He had pushed Darcy against the wall and was holding her

there by her shoulders, his fingers and thumbs digging into her skin. He could tell he was hurting her but paid it no mind. There were more important things to worry about.

"I will never be with you," he growled, bringing his face close to hers. "I don't love you. I don't even know you."

Darcy narrowed her eyes and yanked free of his grip, rubbing her forearms where his hands had been. Archer could see deep red fingerprints beginning to form there.

"Then I'll go to the media and tell them what I saw: you, talking to thin air, wrapping your arms around someone who wasn't even there. I taped it, you know. You didn't see me, but I was there. I recorded the whole thing. You'll become a laughingstock in Hollywood. Is that what you want? For your career to go into the toilet?"

"I really don't give a damn," Archer said, unfazed. "I was thinking about leaving the business anyway. You can go to the press all you want, but remember this: it won't make me love you."

Darcy took a step back, planning her next move. She was down, but not out. He just needed a little more persuasion, that was all. And it came to her before she could even threaten him with it.

"*ARCHER!*" Lucy cried from the basement. "Archer, *be careful!*"

He looked at Darcy with wide eyes and felt every muscle in his body tense up.

"She's here?" he asked.

"See for yourself," Darcy said, and ran for the basement door before he could.

****

Lucy was almost able to lift herself out of the chair when Darcy burst into the basement room and ran over to her with a crazed look on her face. She grabbed Lucy by the hair and yanked her head back, exposing her neck, to which she placed a sharp, cold knife point.

Archer pounded down the stairs and appeared in the doorway with naked panic on his handsome face. Once he saw the knife, he threw his hands up in the air like a man being held up by a mugger and stayed where he was.

"Calm down," he said softly. "I don't even care how you found out about Lucy or how you got her here, I just want everyone to be cool and stay safe." His tongue snaked out and licked his upper lip; suddenly his mouth felt hot and dry and metallic. "You know you can't hurt her, so just don't do anything rash and we'll all get through this just fine."

"Oh, that's right," Darcy said, digging the knife into Lucy's throat. A tiny pinpoint of blood appeared, a crimson dot on the pale skin of her neck, and she whimpered. It had been so long since she had felt pain, and this hurt! Not much more than a bee sting, but still...why was she able to feel so much all of a sudden? "You don't know the latest development."

"What are you talking about?" Archer asked, eying the knife.

"Well, my good friend Mercy--she's upstairs--is something of a chemist. She makes these potions, you see, and they do all sorts of wonderful things. They can make people invisible--which really comes in handy for a girl like me--and they can also bring back the dead."

Archer's breath caught in his throat. His eyes moved from the knife to Lucy's face, where a sudden realization was dawning. "You mean--" he began, and Darcy laughed.

"Yes, I mean," she said. "You guessed it. I figured you would, being a smart guy and all. Your Lucy here is 100% human again. It takes a while for the side effects to wear off, which is why she's sitting here like a bump on a log. But in a few minutes she'll be able to get up and walk around as one of the living. Well, she would, if I wasn't about to slit her throat. And I have to warn you, we're not really sure what happens when a person dies twice."

"NO!" Archer screamed, and before Darcy could make her demands on him, he rushed her.

Several things happened simultaneously:

167

Archer flew across the room at top speed, ready to tackle Darcy in order to wrestle the knife away from her. As he ran, Lucy realized she was able to stand up; her legs still felt heavy, but she could move them just fine. She yanked her head sharply to the right to get out from under the knife and stood up just as Archer reached the chair She angled herself between him and Darcy, who had raised the knife in self defense. Just as Archer raised his hands to knock the weapon from her grip, he realized Lucy had gotten in the way and tried to stop what he knew was going to happen.

He was much too late. Darcy plunged the knife down in an arc, connecting with Lucy's back. Silver points of light flew off the blade as she did so, reminding him crazily of sparklers on the fourth of July. He cried out and caught Lucy as she slumped forward with the knife buried in her back to the hilt. Blood spilled from her mouth and dribbled down the front of her dress, where there was already a spreading dark stain; the knife had knicked her lung.

Darcy looked down at her hands, which were slick with Lucy's blood, and made a thick gagging sound. She had never been able to handle blood; the first time, there hadn't been much of it. This...this was too much. She began to make a low keening sound in the back of her throat, backing away from Archer and Lucy. She turned andran up the stairs, taking them two by two, and when she reached the top she was met not by Mercy, but by a woman she had never seen before.

"You shouldn't have done that," the woman said, and pushed her arms out in front of her in a *shooing* motion. Darcy was thrown back against the wall with such force that one of her shoes flew off and went bouncing down the staircase. She landed with a thud, cracking her tailbone on the baseboard.

"Who are you?" Darcy gasped, rubbing the back of her head. She felt a goose egg rising there and winced.

"My name is Christina, and Archer and Lucy are my friends. You really shouldn't have done that," she repeated.

She threw her arms out again and Darcy felt her feet leave the floor. One moment she was leaning against the wall, and the next she was landing on top of a credenza in the living room, which shattered into a million pieces. Darcy crashed to the floor amongst the wreckage and cowered there. There hadn't even been time to cry out, but when she tried to push herself up with her hands she went right back down with a groan; her arm was broken.

"I'm sorry! Please, no more! I didn't mean to!" she screamed.

"Darcy? What's going on?"

It was Mercy, finally coming downstairs to see what the racket was. She stood on the landing and peered down at the woman who stood over Darcy with murder in her eyes.

"Who are you?" Mercy asked, unable to keep the wobble out of her voice. She was weak and trembly and had broken out in a cold sweat even though she was burning up. Her right arm had that peculiar tight feeling again.

"That's none of your concern," Christina said. "What's important right now is that you and your friend leave this place, right now, and never come back. If you do, I'll come find you. And you won't like that."

"You're dead," Mercy said matter-of-factly. And then, aprapou of nothing: "Smoky hasn't had his medicine today."

With that, Mercy collapsed as her heart finally gave out. She tumbled down the stairs and rolled to a stop not five feet from Darcy, who stared at her in horror.

"Mercy? *Mercy!*" Darcy cried.

"It's too late," Christina said. "Now get out of here." And then, when Darcy didn't get up right away: "*Now.*"

Darcy stood up shakily, using her one good hand for leverage, and when she wasn't quick enough Christina flung her hand towards a bookcase and sent it flying across the room, where it hit a wall and exploded not four feet from where Darcy stood. She screamed and sprinted out the door.

Smoky the cat, who was getting on in years, wasn't quite fast enough to escape the falling debris. He collapsed beneath a pile of wood with a weak yelp, where he was forgotten.

Christina watched Darcy go with fury in her eyes and in her

169

heart, her hands shaking with the effort of controlling it enough to keep from killing the girl. She turned toward the staircase and made her way slowly to the basement.

****

She found Archer kneeling on the floor in the main room, cradling Lucy's head in his lap. He was rocking back and forth and sobbing over her; she was laying perfectly still with her eyes closed. Her long, dark hair trailed along the floor, the tips glistening with blood.

"I'm so, so sorry I was late," she said softly, placing a hand on his shoulder. "I tried to get here as quickly as I could when I realized what was happening."

He didn't acknowledge her, just kept rocking and crying, crying and rocking.

"It's not your fault, you know," she said, and he turned so quickly on her that she actually stepped back.

"Yes it is," he said through his teeth. "It's completely my fault. Just go away, I don't want to hear your comforting words right now. Nothing you say will make me feel better."

"What if I told you that Lucy is awake?" she asked, gesturing to Lucy, who was indeed awake and staring up at Archer in confusion.

"Oh, my God," he whispered, and leaned down to cover her face with kisses. "Oh, Lucy, you're okay!"

"What happened?" she asked groggily. "Did something just happen?"

Archer laughed through his tears and helped her sit upright, wrapping his arms around her so tightly she couldn't move.

"Yes, several things happened," he said, swiping at his eyes with the back of his hand. "Like you saving my life, for starters."

Lucy looked down at herself, at the blood staining her dress, and then a gleam of silver caught her eye. It was the knife, stained with red and laying discarded halfway across the room, where Archer had thrown it after gently pulling it out of her back.

"I did, didn't I?" she said softly, reaching around to touch the wound she knew was there. But instead of torn flesh, there was only a shredded dress.

"Your skin feels the same as it always has," Archer marveled, running his fingertips over her arm. The contact made her shiver. "When Darcy stabbed you, she killed you, and you went right back to the way you used to be."

"I think so," Lucy said. "I feel...different."

He turned to Christina. "What happened up there?"

"I asked Darcy and her friend to leave. Very politely, of course."

"It sounded like you maimed her."

"She'll be fine. Unfortunately, her friend wasn't so lucky. But she didn't die by my hands. She had a heart attack."

"Oh no," Lucy said suddenly. "You're talking about Mercy? The older lady?"

Christina nodded. "She was the one responsible for the potion which made you human again."

Tears welled up in Lucy's eyes and she looked down at her hands as the room blurred. "I know. And now I'll never know how she made it."

Archer cupped her cheek in his hand. "It's okay. We don't need it."

"But it would make things so much easier, Archer, you don't understand--"

He shook his head. "I understand. But it doesn't matter. I have you here, now, and that's all I want. You saved my life, Lucy. Do you realize how amazing that is? That's why you and I were meant to meet, I think. It was fate."

She looked up at him then, at the earnest look in his eyes, and smiled. "I think maybe you're right."

"We should go," Christina said softly. "There are other things which need our attention."

Archer stood up and helped Lucy carefully to her feet, wrapping his muscular forearm around her waist for support. They climbed the stairs slowly, although there was no need;

Lucy felt physically fine, other than the whole being dead thing.

"Wow, Christina," Archer said as they reached the top of the staircase. He surveyed the damage to the living room and let out a low whistle. "You must have really done a number on Darcy."

"Nothing she didn't deserve," Christina muttered, leading the way to the door through the debris.

Archer and Lucy followed in her path, and suddenly something occured to Archer. He stopped in his tracks and Lucy, who was holding his hand, stopped with him.

"How did you get here?" he asked Christina. "I thought you couldn't leave the farm."

Christina turned around and smiled, and Archer saw something he hadn't noticed before now; she was changed in an almost unnameable way. It took him a moment to figure out what it was, and then he realized that her smile wasn't so sad anymore. She looked genuinely happy for the first time since he had known her.

"Dean is gone," she said happily. "I don't know where he went and I don't care. All I know is that I don't feel his presence at all anymore. It's different than before, when I felt him leave but knew he would come back....now there's just peace on that farm. I think maybe he finally decided to stay wherever it is he's been traveling to. And that's fine with me."

"He was keeping you there, wasn't he?" Lucy asked softly. "That's why you've been using those Egyptian symbols, for protection."

Christina nodded and Archer looked at Lucy in awe.

"He found a spell in some old book someplace, a binding spell. As long as he called that farm home, I was unable to leave. I tried several times, but it was almost as though an invisible barrier was keeping me on the property. The only thing I could do was use those symbols to keep him from doing me any harm. I found them in the same book he got the binding spell from. I was never able to find anything I could use against him, but what I did find was useful enough. The charms kept him at bay and allowed me to control when you could leave when one of us called you into a dream."

"Why didn't you ever tell me? I could have helped you," Archer said.

"It wasn't your problem," Christina said simply. "I didn't want to burden you with it, or get you involved."

He turned to Lucy. "How did you know--"

She shrugged. "Women's intuition, I guess."

But it was a little more than that, she thought. Ever since Christina had touched her cheek and proclaimed her to be a "good soul", Lucy had felt a vague connection with her. Perhaps it was the fact that they shared an affection for Archer; perhaps simply that they were two female spirits who had similar energies. Lucy wasn't sure, but it was nice to feel a connection with someone else. She felt sure that she and Christina would become good friends.

"Come, let's leave," Christina said. "We can use the phone at the house to call someone about Mercy. It isn't right to just leave her here."

Archer and Lucy nodded their agreement and followed her to the door. But just as they were about to leave, a small moan came from somewhere in the room.

Lucy whipped her head around in alarm. "Do you think Mercy is still alive?"

Christina shook her head. "Impossible. She would have broken her neck from the fall down the stairs even if the heart attack hadn't killed her."

The three of them were silent for a moment, and then the moan came again, from beneath a pile of wreckage in a far corner of the room.

Archer took Lucy's hand and they made their way cautiously to the source of the sound. The scattered remnants of what looked like a bookshelf lay haphazardly across the floor, and it was from beneath this that the sounds were coming.

Archer began to lift pieces of wood, tossing them to the side one by one, and Lucy joined in cautiously. Christina stood where she was by the door, ready to step in if they needed her.

It took several moments, but soon enough a man's hand was visible; then an arm; then part of a torso. They moved faster, careful not to put pressure on any of the boards in case the man was seriously injured. And finally, he was fully uncovered.

Archer stepped back and looked at him--a painfully thin man lying curled up in the fetal position, no clothing to cover his nudity--and wondered who he was and how he had gotten there. He was still unconscious, but his fingers twitched at his side as though he was in the throes of a bad dream.

Lucy suddenly swayed on her feet as her vision began to blur. The room danced away from her as the ceiling traded places with the wall; she slumped gracefully against Archer's side and he caught her before she fell to the floor, then slid to his knees and supported her head in his lap.

"Christina?" he cried in alarm, but she was already at his side.

She knelt down and brushed Lucy's hair from her eyes.

"It's alright, she's only fainted," she said with a frown.

"I don't understand..." he began, but as he looked again at the man in front of him, he thought maybe he did understand...though not fully. He had seen that face somewhere before: in Lucy's locket.

"Ben?" he whispered.

Epilogue

Darcy trudged slowly up the road, holding her injured arm against her chest as she did so. Her head was pounding, she was bleeding from half a dozen little cuts on her face, and her ankle felt twisted. And now, thanks to some meddling bitch of a ghost, she had no money and no Mercy to help her out. She had left everything at the house, including her cell phone. She couldn't call a cab even if she had the means and the funds; she had no idea where she was. She had been walking forever, and the day was overcast. It would be just her luck to have to walk into town in the pouring rain.

She mourned the loss of Mercy, but even more so, the loss of Archer. He had been her one true love, and somehow everything had gotten screwed up so *badly*. She still wasn't entirely sure how it had all gone so wrong, but she knew one thing; she had to somehow make it back home to Virginia and retrieve Mercy's notes, despite the dead man who was probably still wandering the streets looking for her. Now that she was on her own, she would have to make the most of it and get straight to work.

"Excuse me," a man's voice said from behind her.

She turned to find a rather handsome cowboy standing in the road, looking at her kindly, and smiled in spite of her pain. Maybe he could help her.

"Are you okay, miss?" he asked.

Darcy sighed in relief. "Not really," she said, walking towards him. "Could you give me a ride into town? I need to get to a hospital."

"Sure thing, Miss...?"

"Darcy," she said, trying her best to look pitiful. Maybe if he felt sorry for her he would buy her dinner. But there was something odd about him, she realized as she looked into his eyes; they were so dark they were almost black. It was as if his pupils were dialated, but she knew that wasn't it; it was just the way they were. "Just Darcy," she said.

175

"Well, Just Darcy," he said, putting an arm gently around her shoulders and steering her back the way she had come. "I'm Dean. It's a pleasure to meet you."

Epilogue, Part 2

Page from a journal, found among Mercy Daniels' belongings:

I can't see my reflection in the water. It seems like it's been months--or maybe years--since I last saw the sight of my own nose and eyes and lips, but time, it means nothing here in the Delta. The days are slow with heat and the nights are humid and lonely, and if the sun didn't show its face every now and then I'd have no comprehension of time passing.

The last thing I really remember is the roar, the sonic rush of noise against my eardrums as I fought to keep that weight off my chest. Now I can't remember what caused that weight, that bucket of bricks that made its home on my lungs. I stopped breathing and every memory I had seemed to fly out of my mind as the last exhalation I would ever make slipped between my parted lips.

But that's not entirely true. Some memories won't go away, no matter how hard I try to forget: memory of my mother the last time I saw her, the day I broke her heart. Her faded housedress with its pattern of rosebuds, auburn hair streaked through with gray, laugh lines around her eyes and stress lines around her mouth. The way she looked when I was leaving, standing in our dooryard with shoulders rounded as though with defeat. My baby sister Emily as she was when she was little; curls the rich color of honey and eyes full of mischief and tiny hands reaching for me to pick her up. All these things have burned themselves upon my eyes and printed their image on my heart.

And it's not as though these are bad memories, far from it. They are simply too full of the people and things I love. The people I had to leave behind. I think of James suddenly and wonder if he's distraught that I'm gone. I wonder if he's written a song about me yet. His voice was always so beautiful, so full of sorrow when he sang. It is what drew me to him, made me want to take care of him. He used to say that a happy musician would never be able to write songs. I suppose now he's able to write all the songs he wants.

Here is something else I cannot forget: the way his skin smelled and tasted first thing in the morning, sleep-warm and soft, softer than any man's skin has a right to be. I would be sure to wake up before him just so I could roll over and kiss the tender flesh of his shoulder, wrap my arm around his waist and pull myself into the curve of his back. Smell the clean scent of him and taste the salt of his skin. I never tired of the taste/scent of him; I couldn't get enough. On the nights we were apart I couldn't sleep unless I had one of his old t-shirts in the bed with me. I'd put it up to my face and inhale him. Smoke and soap and something indefinable, something that was simply James.

He used to say I had the prettiest legs of any girl he'd ever met. It could be my naivete, but I heard a ring of truth in those words. I guess in those days he could have told me just about anything and I would have believed him. He's the kind of guy, you'll take his word for gospel even when it's ridiculous. Even when it's the word love.

We met in a bar. I know, it's almost too cliché for words, but it's not what you think. I wasn't there to pick myself up a husband. I was only nineteen, keep in mind, and it was summer. The smell of freshly cut grass drew everyone out of their homes, pulled as if by magnetic force to the sweet night air and the lightning bugs that filled it. I, like almost everyone else in town, was in the mood to celebrate life.

At any rate, he was the dark, brooding guy at the end of the bar with the melancholy eyes and pouty lips that girls like me die for. I stood and watched him for a little bit; the way he nursed his beer, as though he'd had too much to drink the night before, the way the sleeves on his plaid shirt were rolled up to the elbows so they wouldn't get in the way when he played guitar. I hadn't seen him on stage, but I knew his type: the wounded man with the haunting voice who played guitar the way most men touch a woman. With love and reverence. I stood in the shadows and watched a scene play out in my head. He would get up any minute and play his set and I would introduce myself after, the polite girl who never did things like this, never chatted up strange men in bars. In fact, to this day I have no idea what brought me to that place--McKinley's on Rose Street--on that specific night. Oh, I had been there many times before, but that night was different.

I was alone, for one thing, which was unusual. My best friend Julia was tending to her sick mama and all of my other girlfriends were out on dates. I thought of what my own mama would say if she knew where I was and smiled just to spite her, as though she could see me. I'd had a fake ID since I was seventeen and I was always careful to go to the bars in the bigger--more anonymous--surrounding towns of Bartlett or Collierville, where I wouldn't be recognized.

I suppose I had just wanted to get out of the house for a bit, to revel in the freedom that came with going to a bar alone and in the feeling that I wasn't out to impress. I'd gone with the notion that I didn't need anyone, yet by the time the night was through I had found the only man I would ever need, the man I would at times physically yearn for.

I sipped my beer and watched the muscles jump in his forearms as he flexed his hands to prepare for the set. I wondered what it would be like to kiss those arms, feel those muscles tremble beneath my lips.

He looked at me suddenly, as though he had heard my thoughts, and I turned away before he could see how flushed my cheeks were. I had never had thoughts like those before, not even about Gray Burgess, and we'd dated for two years in high school. With him it was easy to forget about romance. Everything was his way, what he wanted, and if I was lucky my pleasure would come as an afterthought. Toward the end when I looked at him all I could see was the man he would become, beaten down by this little town and by his inability to be all the things his parents wanted him to be. He would be a heavy drinker, a big man with football muscles turned to fat, beer gut straining the waistband of his pants, knuckles grimed with motor oil and fists quick to lash out at the woman unfortunate enough to marry him. And perhaps the saddest thing would be the way you could look at his face and see the handsome boy who used to be there, buried beneath the years and the disappointment.

But this man, this guitar-playing heartbreaker, he was different. I could see it in the way he raised the beer bottle to his lips and in the slow smile that spread across his face when I dared to peek at him again from behind the curtain of my long dark hair. He was not a man who would hurt a woman, at least not on purpose. He was not a man who would drink his life away when it didn't go the way he'd planned it. He was a man who would kiss the woman he loved for hours, until her lips were bruised and used-looking. He was a man who would play his guitar on the front porch after sunset and sing a lullaby to the Evening Primrose plants blooming around him.

I listened to him play that night and I knew from the first song that I was in love. His voice was deep and resonated with a sadness I'd thought was only in my heart until then. I watched his fingers move on the guitar neck and closed my eyes, wishing they were on me instead. When he switched his acoustic guitar for a slide, I moved from my spot at the bar to a table near the front and listened with my whole heart as my beer grew first warm and then flat. I didn't care. I was in love.

After his set was over he went backstage for a while and emerged with damp hair and a different shirt. I figured the other one was soaked with sweat; the stage lights were hot and bright and he had played for almost two hours. The crowd kept wanting more, and every time he tried to play the "last song" someone would request something else. He seemed unable to turn them down, as though ignoring their love for his music would make it go away. The patrons at the bar seemed to know him well, and there wasn't a song title they shouted out that wasn't in his repertoire.

He played Elvis. He played The Allman Brothers. He played Johnny Cash. He played beautiful, haunting melodies that I understood to be his own. Each song seemed to come from someplace deep inside him, some well that held memories and music notes all tangled up together.

When he took a seat at the end of the bar once more I waited for his fans to come congratulate him on the good set. I watched as he received claps on the back from the men and kisses on the cheek from the women, one of whom was a frankly bleached blond who was probably a grandmother. Her mini skirt rode up a full two inches when she bent to kiss him, a good hard smack on the mouth that caught her husband's attention. He actually half-rose from his seat to pull her away but was stopped by a drunken friend with a story to tell.

Everyone in a bar past midnight has a story, have you ever noticed that? Funny, sad, disgusting, romantic, they all roll into one after a while. Not that I am a seasoned bar-fly, not at all. It's just that I am a people-watcher and I notice these things. It doesn't matter how disinterested the other person is, the storyteller will keep going even when he knows it could turn out bad for him. Why is that? Why do we do that to ourselves? Is it out of some base need to connect with someone else, even if it's just for five minutes in a dimly lit pub? Drunken words slur together until they are unintelligible over the sounds of the juke or the band or the cries of the waitress for another round on her tray and still we go on, trying like hell to tell the one story or joke that might bring us closer to another person for the night.

I didn't have a story. I bought a beer and sent it over to him and waited. And when he moved to sit beside me I kept my eyes on the bar, traced the rings on the wood made by many, many beer bottles over the years as though I could discover how old it was by those rings.

"Bartender says you sent this over," he said, and I dared to look up at him through my bangs.

"Yes," I said softly. "I wanted to thank you."

181

"Thank me?" His dark eyes regarded me thoughtfully, a small smile playing at his lips.

"For the music. I feel like now I've heard it I can die a happy girl."

The smile fell away so quickly I was afraid I'd upset him, but he only patted my hand like I was his niece or a family member he was trying to console.

"Come with me," he said, and I was happy enough to follow him out the back door. We took our beers with us. No one seemed to mind.

Outside the night was hot but bright with moonlight and the stars were winking at us as though they knew secrets mere mortals did not. We sat on the back stoop and his knee grazed mine and I found that I didn't even mind that the dumpsters were nearby.

"I'm James, by the way," he said softly. His voice was much the same as it had been onstage, deep and melodic with a touch of sadness. I wondered if he carried that sadness with him all the time or if something had happened to him earlier in the night.

"I know," I said, smiling a little. "I'm Charly."

He looked a bit surprised at that and I rolled my eyes. "My dad was a big Charlie Daniels fan. You can imagine his disappointment when I was born a girl."

He laughed and it was one of those good, whole-body laughs that let me know he wasn't laughing at me or my situation but rather *with* me.

"He couldn't have been all that disappointed, he still named you after his favorite musician."

"Well I can't play the fiddle to save my life and that used to irritate him some. He could play just about any instrument he picked up, but mostly he played banjo with a band called The Pickers and The Grinners. They toured around the south for a while when I was a girl, playing little dives, but they could pack a house. He would have done it for free if it hadn't been for me and my mama at home, needin' an income. He loved it that much."

"And he wanted you to be a part of the band?" he asked, partially joking.

"I guess he thought when I got to be old enough we'd be like some crazy country version of The Partridge Family."

He smiled at that and looked up toward the sky, as if waiting for something to appear there.

"Listen, I asked you to come out here because I wanted to actually get to know you," he said finally.

That was the beginning.

****

I picture him as I sit on the bank of the Mississippi, wishing I had a cigarette. I watch the muddy water rush past me as though it has someplace to be and think of all the things I wanted to do and be when I was just a girl growing up in Memphis. I think of my father, my mother, my sister. And I think of the man I still love, even through the boundaries of time and space. The boundaries of life.

The boundaries of death.

I'm dead.

My name is Charly Owens and I am dead.

It's the first time I've allowed that word to form itself in my mind. I turn it over and roll it over my tongue, as though tasting it. Dead. Death.

I really wish I had a cigarette.

And I really wish I could place the image I have of a girl with long dark hair standing over me, her face distorted by the weight of water over my head.